Additional Praise for

The Assassination of Margaret Thatcher

A *New York Times* Bestseller

Named a Best Fiction Book of the Year by
The New York Times Book Review
Los Angeles Times • *The Washington Post*
Amazon • Barnes & Noble • *Kirkus Reviews*
The Independent (London) • *The Telegraph* (London)
The Guardian (London)

"Mantel's stories have their own special tang and quidditas. Even as one appreciates the suave authorial style—light, pared-down, technically scintillating, like the Olympic gymnast who nails her landing every time—one has the sense too that Mantel is working with some fairly edgy and complex private material in these contemporary fables. . . . One gets the feeling she wants both to frighten us (at times more than a little) *and* make us laugh." —*The New York Times Book Review*

"Heads always tend to roll—figuratively and otherwise—in Mantel's writing. Hers is a brusque and brutal world leavened with humor—humor that's available in one shade only: black. . . . Makes a permanent dent in a reader's consciousness because of Mantel's striking language and plot twists, as well as the Twilight Zone–type mood she summons up. . . . Breathtaking."

—Maureen Corrigan, NPR

"[Mantel's] writing is cinematically exquisite. . . . You can't help but get sucked in." —*Chicago Tribune*

"*The Assassination of Margaret Thatcher* delivers on its promises: the promise built by Mantel's reputation as one of the unquestionably great contemporary writers, the promise made by its shocking title, and the promise inherent in the genre of short stories." —*A.V. Club*

"A little sweet treat . . . Some of the stories are so brief and twisted . . . they have a hint of the cruelty of Roald Dahl's short stories (the ones that were definitely for grown-ups)." —*USA Today* (four stars)

"Here is the Mantel of her earlier, darker kitchen-sink novels: harsh and comic, even derisive."

—*Los Angeles Times*

"[Mantel] evokes a shadowy region where boundaries blur and what might have happened has equal weight with what actually occurred. . . . Even the most straight-forward of Mantel's tales retains a faintly otherworldly air."

—*The Washington Post*

"A barnburner of a title story . . . It's not the plot that matters as much as the superb little touches with which Ms. Mantel punctuates it."   —*The New York Times*

"Hilary Mantel has escaped from King Henry VIII's court."   —*The Wall Street Journal*

"[Mantel is] an international literary star."   —*Elle*

"One of the best novelists writing today."

—*Entertainment Weekly*

"Mantel's new story collection pulls us into an atmosphere as claustrophobic and unsafe as any imagined by the Bronte sisters. . . . This is brilliant, subversive writing, the perfect fix for those waiting for the third book in Mantel's Wolf Hall trilogy." —*More*

"On hearing that there was to be a new book by Hilary Mantel this year, pulses quickened. . . . [A] masterly collection of stories." —*Minneapolis Star Tribune*

"Perfect." —*San Francisco Chronicle*

"Mantel is not just a novelist, however, but a great political novelist at the top of her game." —*Salon*

"Genius." —*The Seattle Times*

"The stories are artfully constructed and share a muted Gothic tone marked by the same 'heightened, crawling quality' that one of Mantel's narrators, a writer, finds at a moldering hotel." —*The New Yorker*

"Untied from the historical record, she gives her characters freer rein to rattle their chains . . . satisfyingly chilling."   —*The Daily Beast*

"Behind fiction's door, Mantel shows, anything can happen; and in the mind's eye, perhaps it already has."
                                          —*The Christian Science Monitor*

"Here are stories in which horror shudders between the high Gothic of Grimm and the menacing quotidian. . . . These are Ms. Mantel's signature strokes—freaks made human and humans made freakish, and always with the expiation of a dark and judgmental humor."
                                          —*Pittsburgh Post-Gazette*

"Quirky, unsettling . . . Mantel's fictional worlds are pervaded by menace, her characters beset by infidelity, illness, loneliness, and sometimes the uncanny."
                                          —*The Kansas City Star*

"The atmosphere throughout is creepy, alarming, and unsettling. In other words, just wonderful! Mood and plot merge into incredible scenarios that ultimately and disturbingly end up seeming to be perfectly natural. . . . Unforgettable surprises and pleasures await."

—*Booklist* (starred review)

"This is a brilliant example of short fiction." —*Guernica*

"Brilliant . . . You'll have a hard time finding a smarter selection this season or any." —*Refinery 29*

"With ten stories unique, strange, and tantalizing, Mantel shares her views poetically, harshly, and with great love. A have-to-read." —*Bustle*

"Undeniably beautifully crafted and well executed . . . This is Hilary Mantel at her best."

—*New York Journal of Books*

THE
ASSASSINATION
OF
MARGARET
THATCHER

STORIES

HILARY MANTEL

PICADOR

A JOHN MACRAE BOOK

HENRY HOLT AND COMPANY

NEW YORK

THE ASSASSINATION OF MARGARET THATCHER. Copyright © 2014, 2015
by Tertius Enterprises Ltd. All rights reserved. Printed in the
United States of America. For information, address Picador,
175 Fifth Avenue, New York, N.Y. 10010.

www.picadorusa.com
www.twitter.com/picadorusa • www.facebook.com/picadorusa
picadorbookroom.tumblr.com

Picador® is a U.S. registered trademark and is used by
Henry Holt under license from Pan Books Limited.

For book club information, please visit www.facebook.com/picadorbookclub
or e-mail marketing@picadorusa.com.

An extension of this copyright page appears on page 289.

Designed by Meryl Sussman Levavi

The Library of Congress has cataloged the Henry Holt edition as follows:

Mantel, Hilary, 1952–
    [Short stories. Selections]
    The assassination of Margaret Thatcher: stories / Hilary Mantel.—
First U.S. edition.
        p. cm.
    "A John Macrae book."
    ISBN 978-1-62779-210-3 (hardcover)
    ISBN 978-1-62779-211-0 (e-book)
    I. Mantel, Hilary, 1952– —Sorry to Disturb.   II. Title.
    PR6063.A438A6 2014
    823'.914—dc23

                                                    2014015900

Picador Paperback ISBN 978-1-250-07472-0

Picador books may be purchased for educational, business, or promotional use. For
information on bulk purchases, please contact the Macmillan Corporate and Premium Sales
Department at 1-800-221-7945, extension 5442, or write to specialmarkets@macmillan.com.

Published simultaneously in Great Britain by Fourth Estate

First published in the United States by Henry Holt and Company, LLC

First Picador Edition: September 2015

10 9 8 7 6 5 4 3 2 1

To Bill Hamilton,

the man in William IV Street:

thirty years on, with gratitude

CONTENTS

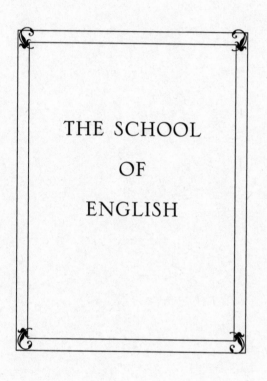

THE SCHOOL

OF

ENGLISH

Lastly," Mr. Maddox said, "and to conclude our tour, we come to a very special part of the house." He paused, to impress on her that she was going to have a treat. "Perhaps, Miss Marcella, it may be that in your last situation, the house did not have a panic room?"

Marcella put her hand to her mouth. "God help them. The family go in together, or one at a time?"

"There is capacity for all the family," Mr. Maddox said. "The need arising, which God forbid."

"Which God forbid," she repeated. The idea of group agitation . . . how, she wondered, does panic ignite and spread? Is it parents to children, children to parents? "Can the doctor do nothing for them?" she asked. "There are pills to stop fear. Also they say, breathe into a paper bag. It does good in some way, I am not sure how."

Mr. Maddox—the butler—turned his eyes on her, and she knew she had made an error. Perhaps she had shown over-familiarity. Or perhaps she had mistaken his meaning; this seemed likely. "So it is not," she said tentatively, "a room you go in when you are frightened?"

"It is not a mere room," Mr. Maddox said, "but a facility. Follow and I will show you." But he turned back. "If you were making a joke, I heartily discourage you. I myself benefitted from the care of English nursery teacher. I am joking like a native speaker. But in such exclusive postcodes as St. John's Wood, or in any leafy part of this great metropolis, it is easy to give offense." He patted the paunch beneath his T-shirt. (We are a modern, informal household, she had been told.) "Miss Marcella," he said, "come with me."

She would never have guessed the door they passed through was a door at all. It seemed like mere wall. Once it was opened, the light came on by itself, and it showed a part of the house that was concealed except to those who were, like the butler, in the know: that was where he said he was.

"Mr. Maddox," she said, "I am to clean here?"

"Weekly," he said. "Vacuum, air freshener, toilet clean. Even if never used."

"Which God forbid it should be," she said. She looked around her and began to understand the panic room. Mr. Maddox showed her the big bottles of water and the cupboard with its supply of snack food. There was a sofa and two chairs, covered in a business-like charcoal fabric; they looked hard and could have used some cushions. There was a lavatory with a cold block of soap, a supermarket soap inferior to that in the rest of the house. Why? she wondered. Why sink your standards of comfort? She saw how, from week to week, the green lavatory cleaner in the unflushed bowl would pool, a verdant lake deepening.

Against the far wall there was a single bed with a frame of tubular metal, made up with starched white sheets and a navy blue blanket tucked in tight. "Only one to sleep?" she asked.

"Sleep is not envisaged," the butler said. "Within an hour, and please God within less, either the police or the security service will liberate. The bed is for a casualty."

"Sorry," Marcella said. "I don't know this word."

She had irritated Mr. Maddox. "I thought you came here via The Lady. And good English guaranteed thereby."

"The Lady is not my employer," Marcella said. "It is only a means to an end." She stopped and wondered at the phrase: "a means to an end." She said, "I am English-tested. In my bag here I have a certificate."

"I do not give a fig for your certificate," Mr. Maddox snapped. "As for The Lady, I know it is not your employer. Do not trifle. I repeat: I believed that only a person of great excellence in the English language would peruse The Lady."

"No." Marcella began to feel tired. She thought she would like to stretch out on the panic room's metal bed. She had seen worse beds, and some of them across the town, in Notting Hill. "The Lady is freely available to all seeking domestic work," she said. "It is only a magazine. It is not the works of Alfred Lord Tennyson. It is not a manual of magic spells."

"Impertinence will not carry you far," the butler said. "Only by a short route to dismissal, and no employment tribunal for you, do not think it. Her Majesty's Government in its wisdom is pleased to remove legal aid from you whinging type of person. So once dismissed they stay dismissed. I am warning you."

The floor of the panic room struck cold into Marcella's feet. The salary promised was small, but she needed a roof over her head, and here was that roof: NW8, live-in, for flexible person must like dogs, with experience of specialist laundry and helpful attitude, non-smoker. At a good distance north of here, there was a room over a fried chicken shop, where certain of her countrywomen gathered and passed The Lady hand to hand, as if they had never reached the age of the internet: they were not digital, they could not recharge, they were unable to keep a laptop in case it was filched from their very laps, or any portable device that simply added to what they had to carry; they feared street robbers. The Lady, therefore, scanned by so many eyes, became limp and grey; it became circled in red, crossed in green, starred in blue. In the room above the deep-fat fryers, a woman might conceal herself from officers, police or other types: hiding if she was wanted, hiding if she was unwanted—that is to say, dismissed. She might resort there for a night or more, if she had no alternative but the streets. Sometimes the women lay end to end, exhausted, rolled into sleeping bags or blankets, grey faces vacant in sleep; when they woke, they hardly knew their own names.

So it was with a look both humble and contrite that Marcella made her apology to Mr. Maddox. "I only asked the meaning of a word. In future I shall buy a dictionary."

"Well, you are young," the butler conceded. "Perhaps you may yet learn. 'Casualty' is an injured person. Gunshot wound for example."

She could see such a person would need to lie down. "Who has shot them?"

"Intruder. Kidnapper. Abductor. Robber. Outrager. Terrorist. Desperado."

"Peril on every side," Marcella murmured.

"This is a very basic panic room," the butler explained. "A bullet will not pierce it, and the air, being filtered, is able to eliminate most chemicals and biologicals, but it is designed to accommodate only till the security men comes at the touch of a button. I mean, the panic buttons," he instructed. "They are placed in all living areas."

"Are they red?"

"Red? Why would they be?"

"How shall I know them? If I do not spot them I might press them when I am dusting, at a time when there is no terrorist threat, and this can lead to The Boy Who Cried Wolf."

The butler stared at her. As she suspected, though his English was more florid than hers, his range of allusion was less.

"Of course they are not red," he said. "They are concealed so our employers can press them discreetly. They are in hidden places."

"But I must dust them," Marcella said, "hidden or not. I was recently in Notting Hill, where I was dismissed for failing to dust the chair legs."

"That cannot have been your only fault." Mr. Maddox

said. He spoke as if weighing the matter, and his tone was dubious. "In Kensington, certainly. In Holland Park, perhaps. In Notting Hill? I doubt it. You had better be open with me. What else did you do? Or should I say, what did you omit to do?"

"I was not raped," Marcella said. "I consented."

THE CIRCUMSTANCES WERE simple and they were these. The family—that is to say, her previous family, in Notting Hill—had left for ski break. The child Jonquil was taken out of school, but Joshua, who was fifteen years old, was left behind, either because he was not worthy of ski break, or because it was his exam year, Marcella has now forgotten; there was a row about it in the kitchen, during which Joshua dropped a glass jar of multigrain multiseed on the floor, and this she remembers because of the complaints made for days after, about gritty grains under bare soles. The upshot was that his mother said, we are going for ski break, Joshua, even if you throw the whole of Waitrose breakfast aisle on the floor. You do what you like, Marcella will clear it up. You may get your chance another year, may I remind you we are a hard-working family and we deserve it.

Later, as she was climbing to her room, she found Joshua sitting on the stairs and crying. He was a huge, thick-bodied boy, and it seemed he was using up all the air, his big face wet with tears, his breath heaving in and out. It was her personal stairs he was sitting on; no reason for him to be there; his room was below, second floor. "Don't look at me," he said.

She understood he was ashamed of crying, such a large boy. But why did he come there, if not for her to look at him?

She said, "Do not snivel, Joshua." She meant it kindly, but she saw him stiffen. Perhaps the wrong word? "Sniffle, I mean," she said. "Do not do either. There will be other ski breaks."

"It's not my fault my mother fucked off and left me with *her*," he said. Left me with a stepmother, he meant. "But it's always me that has to be punished for it. Why's that, then?"

He did not expect her to have an answer. And yet she did. She said gently, "When you are punished, Joshua, it is not always because you have been bad. Often it is because others have been bad."

She waited. He was not intelligent. He did not understand her. "The sooner you know this, the better for you," she said. "It is not just, of course."

"Not just what?" He was staring at her.

"It is not . . ." Irritation bubbled inside her, and swelled inside her mouth like a balloon. Always she tried to feel sorry for him. But perhaps if he did not take up so much room, and if he were more hygienic. "I mean to say, it is not fair. But it is the way things are. Now, hurry. Your father is waiting to take you back to school. Among your laughing comrades you will soon forget your miseries."

Joshua hoisted his bulk to the vertical. "Why are you so full of crap?"

"Your bag is in the car and I have put your chocolate raisins in the secret compartment, six packs. Remember to clean your teeth afterwards, for they are not good for your dentition."

He looked down at her. "Move."

I will speak, she thought. It is for his welfare. "Joshua, it is truly said, 'You don't know you are born.' I have learned this expression recently and its meaning is, a person should count its blessings. You are blessed with loving family, in part at least. You have good health and education, warm clothes and laundry, food cooked for you every day of the year, pocket money is given you for nothing, and no work except try to be pleasant and polish your school shoes after long weekend exeat, which always you fail to do. Be a big boy," she said. "Only child cries over ski break. A baby, the age of Jonquil. For you, Joshua, it is time to be a man."

Joshua had no handkerchief, despite her laundering. She had never seen him with a handkerchief. In case of need, as now, he wiped his nose on his sleeve. He pushed past her, not looking at her, and clumped downstairs. Every provision for tears is made, she thought, but it is the privilege of the employer and his family to snivel in the wrong way at the wrong time to the wrong person.

On the day the ski break began, once she was sure

the family had left for the airport and could not come back, she stood in the kitchen and treated herself to a proper cup of coffee, just one. She drank it standing up, as if that made the offense less. It was made from a colored pod, and for some time her fingers had hovered over the pod box, choosing which color to have. Acid and thin, the coffee disappointed her. But the ritual, the moment of ease: that did not disappoint. She left the pod on the worktop, glowing like a sapphire on the granite.

She had made a list of all outstanding matters to be achieved before ski break was over, and it ran to two pages, but for the next six days her time was her own to arrange. For an hour or so after the family's departure, their voices seemed to echo and reverberate through the house, but then silence stole through the rooms, and she went upstairs, to the attic floor, and closed her door.

The window of the attic was high, but a cute little window she always thought. On her first day, she had stood on her chair to look out of it. There was nothing to see but the rooftops of Notting Hill, glistening with rain. There was a mirror in her room, which fronted a wardrobe no wider than a coffin. Hang up one raincoat, one cotton jacket, two work uniforms (blue check overall), and perhaps three other garments, squash them together and it was full. This disturbed her. Did they expect her not to stay long? She hoped to stay long; the fried chicken room had been taken back by the landlord, who wished to sell it, and accordingly accused her countrywomen of keeping a brothel. So now between jobs there was nowhere to go, and the caprice of an employer, even the spite of a nanny or twenty-four-hour porter, could be enough to make her one of those destitute women who lurked by supermarket paladins hoping for unwanted prawn sandwiches. Papers in bag, certificate of English and the rest: bag in hand, bag stolen: this too often was the fate of her countrywomen. Sometimes, taken up by the authorities, they admitted to being each other. Sometimes, if one was too sick to work, another would take her keys and silently admit herself to a strange house, to mop floors and scour bathrooms; swerving past the mopper in her overall, employers did not notice, and smiled impartially as a body with a bucket shrank past them on the stairs.

So it is incumbent, Marcella always said, incumbent to accommodate to whatever accommodation; the wardrobe offering so little opportunity, she had folded her cotton jacket and put it in a drawer. There was a chest of four drawers, and a second chest, which looked like drawers but was not. It was in fact a cabinet. If you opened it, inside was her bed. The cabinet ran on castors, and you needed to hold it firm with one hand while pulling out the bed with the other, gripping a bar and yanking the metal frame. If you did not exert your strength against the cabinet, it wheeled itself across the room, your bed still inside.

So now in the empty house—ski break underway, time stretching before her—she had a decision to make. She wanted to mark her freedom by lying down. But never during daylight hours had she pulled out her bed. She pictured herself lying on the striped mattress. It did not seem right. In order to have a nap she would need to make up the bed with the sheets and quilt she kept folded on her chair. After her nap, would she put it all away again? Or would she leave the linen in place, and resume her life as if this were a rational house, where beds were not kept in cupboards?

She went down another flight of stairs, to the bedroom of her employers. It was as if the lady were still present, a cloud of her strange scent lying heavy on the air. It was hard to think a man slept in this room. She looked at the king-sized expanse of the bed. It was covered by a light quilt, off-white, a sepia pattern faint against it, a paisley swirl in vegetable dye. It looked as if had been washed many times, beaten on stones by a woman standing in a stream. But this was not so, for she herself would fetch it from the dry cleaner, swathed in plastic, when the lady spilled her morning coffee on it, or the child Jonquil, climbing affectionately into her parents' bed, spilled her juice or was sick.

I cannot lie on it, she thought. What if I should pollute? She left the room, closing the door softly to trap inside the scent of roses, basil, and lime. She descended one flight, to the bedroom of the child Jonquil. She lay down on her little bed, the headboard stencilled with sheep. Her eyes rested on the nursery frieze. Softly they closed, on an image of long-lashed calves in a meadow of deepest green. The slaughterhouse was not depicted: unless the frieze stretched out, into new rooms, into unknown houses she would clean, long after she was sacked from this one.

At the sound of a door below, she was startled awake. Her mouth was dry and at first she did not know where she was, or who. Because this was broad day, she had not set alarms, either clock or burglar. She got to her feet. I must confront, she thought. Any despoiler. I must defend above all the panelled study with the fitted furniture on which one must not use spray polish, it is forbidden, only wax; I must defend the wall safe, the hardware, the software; I must defend the calves in the meadow, the sepia quilt. She tottered out to the stairhead. Joshua, the son of the house, was coming up to meet her.

"Joshua? Is it you? I thought you were at school."

He glared up at her. "Obviously not. Moron."

Joshua's trousers slid down around his hips, fell in folds over his huge trainers; it was a style abandoned now on the street, but he and his school chums would stick loyally, for cloistered in Wiltshire half the year they knew no better. Such butter-fed oafs, oozing resentment; they sat in the kitchen smoking, they dropped their ash straight on the floor and laughed, they poked her with their toes and pretended it was by accident as she crept around their ankles with dustpan and brush.

"Are you alone?" she said. "School knows where you are?

It came to her, it is Joshua and his ilk who hook the little calves from the nursery frieze, and bite their heads off without even skinning and roasting. Impossible to imagine, that his infant palms in wonder had ever patted the contours of a painted farmyard, or that his childish gaze had rested on a twirling mobile of bluebirds and dragonflies.

She looked him over. He was blocking the stairs. The number "69" was plastered on his gray marl torso, and the hood of the garment was drawn up so his face shone innocent, pink as ham.

"Do not resent me, Joshua," she said. "You asked for explanation of your punishment. I gave it."

"Make food," he said.

"Very well. I can do that. What would you like?"

"Call me sir."

"No."

"Call me sir."

"It is not right, Joshua. Even your father, who is made Sir by the queen, says "you must call me Mike." '

"I don't care what you call that turd," he said, "but you call me sir or you will be sorry."

"I expect I will be sorry anyway," Marcella said. "I usually am."

THAT NIGHT, SHE heard the sounds of the party below. The smash of shattering glass. The panicked thump, thump of music brutally dragged from its mother, whose name is melody: music wailing and thrashing like an orphan left in a field. What should she do? Joshua had simply not replied to her objections. As if he had not heard her. He had elbowed her aside. She wondered if he really had, or if it was just an expression. Her flesh seemed shaped for his elbow, hollowed; she imagined the bruise. She rehearsed the story she would give to Sir Mike. Mob-handed, and no warning, and bringing strangers; your son has elbowed me aside. What am I to do? In advertising, Sir Mike, you did not state, "sole charge." If you had stipulated, I would have said, who, me, Marcella, control that large boy?

Since she was in this job, roof over her head, not exposed to random street theft, she had a mobile phone, and she could have phoned Sir Mike and the lady: except that her phone was downstairs, inside her bag, which she had left by the coffee machine. She could picture it on the granite worktop, by the sapphire pod; though pod would long ago be lost in the violence. It was a black bag of good quality imitation leather; she had an eye for these things, coming as she did from a country where the people were adept in faking, in the application of false logos and the manufacture of false identities for hardworking citizens going overseas. Why, she wondered, do they not spray the bags with false leather scent? Nothing else is wanting. She could see the bag in her mind's eye, soft and squishy as best leather should be. Inside was fifty pounds. It was her life-savings, which she had been able to make only since she came to this house. She knew the party guests would have robbed it long ago.

By midnight, she had thought, they will fall quiet, go down to the basement to watch porno, I shall then steal down. But at midnight more youths surged in, the music rocked the foundations. Every few minutes, fresh gatecrashers hollered from the garden or barged in at the front door. As they thundered below, security lights flashed from neighborhood gardens, and she felt as if she were trapped, in a distant country, in the long equinoctial of a tropical storm. The eye of the storm passed over her, and pinned her to the white wall of her room, where all the district could see and judge her: clueless, useless. It was ten o'clock when the first partygoers had begun to arrive and, after being elbowed, she had retreated upstairs. It was now 1:30 a.m. Soon, she thought, some of them must fall down, out of exhaustion. Perhaps I shall hear the crash of their fall. Perhaps I may be summoned for cut heads or cardiac resuscitation: for which I have certificates. It struck her that if she were to save a life, any der-eliction of her duty would be excused. The parents of the young life saved would be sure to reward her. Perhaps they would give her a job, even, with a proper bed and a three-day weekend every second week: arrangements making for self-respect and mutual consideration.

She took up a position, vigilant, just outside the door of her room. At the sound of feet coming up, she planned to retreat and draw the bolt. She listened for anything she could pick out, above or below the music's pounding beat. That morning, she had been up at four, for final packing for ski break. It was therefore almost twenty-two hours since she had slept. Despite the racket she must have dozed, still on her feet, her head against the wall. When a police siren sounded, she woke with a start. She took the risk of creeping down a half-flight to the landing, where from a narrow window she could see a slice of the street; and from this angle she saw segments of an ambulance lurch to a halt, and fractions of a youth led towards it, his head dropped and a silver blanket shawled around him, like a magic cape that protects from spells.

It was not Joshua. If she had seen him removed, she might have risked going downstairs to pick her way among the fallen bodies. Any party goers who were still upright would probably not mind her, or even notice her; they would know by her demeanor that she was there to clean. But with Joshua in the house she could not risk it. Now she thought of it, she believed he had hit her. There was a dragging ache in her chest she could not otherwise explain. There was soreness behind it, like a punch: knuckles against her breasts.

Once the police and ambulance had come and gone, there was an uneasy peace: sudden screams cut into it, and the banging of doors. She could listen against this quiet, and interpret: it was more frightening than the noise, which had removed all responsibility to understand what she heard. Against that music, that brute with its alien pulse, no one could oppose a small, human action. But now one must decide. Marcella decided to sleep. She slapped her hand down on the top of the cabinet, and began to remove her bed.

It was space-saving, the lady Sophie had said, on her

first day when she showed her where she would live. Marcella bit back an urge to say, but it is my space, and I would rather not save it, I would rather have a proper bed. "I hope you find it comfortable." The lady looked at her as if she did not like what she saw. "The last Filipina was small-boned."

"I am not Filipina," she said.

"But of course, if there's a problem, do just say."

"There is no problem," she had said; that was the answer the lady wanted to hear.

HER SLEEP, TOWARDS dawn, was uneasy. When she woke it was nine o'clock. In silver light, in another country, ski trip had begun. Here, the rain fell. All that day she did not go down. When she did she would have to clean up the vomit and glass, perhaps the blood. She was sensitive to the noises of the house, experienced in them, being ever-alert not to intrude on the family's privacy. So from signs like the flushing of lavatories, she became aware that several youths remained. The presence of others might offer some protection against Joshua; but then, did she want to meet a gang of them, truculent and still drunk: or worse perhaps than drunk?

Soon the weekend would be over. They must surely have places to be. Parents would expect them, schools. Then she would go down and try to rectify the damage. But first she would eat.

She had taken nothing since her guilty cup of coffee, standing at the counter: the cantucci in a glass jar, she had not dared, though now the thought of almond and orange peel tormented her. There was no food in her room. When she first came to the house she had kept cereal bars, but Sir Mike found them. He had apologized for searching her room in her absence but explained that the last Filipina had agreed to hide Joshua's stash of drugs, so they found it wise to perform random searches every few days.

"But I would never hide drugs," she had said.

Sophie, the lady, had said, "He gave the last girl no choice." She said to Sir Mike, "He can be very persuasive, your son."

"His son?" Marcella had queried. "He is not your son also, lady?"

"Good God, how old do you think I am?"

"Forty," Marcella said, truthfully.

"She fucked off to Vancouver!" the lady shouted. "His own mother. She left him. She couldn't stand the sight of him, so now I've got him, for the rest of my life."

Marcella was bemused. Is it possible that the wife had made this journey mentioned, not on purpose to leave her husband, but in order to leave Joshua? Did people run away from their own children? She would have thought it impossible, till she came to this family. "I have led sheltered life," she admitted. She turned to Sir Mike, a question on her lips, but he said, "Marcella, if you wouldn't mind, and I say this more in sorrow than in anger, would you not keep those cereal bars in your room? It encourages vermin."

"Also," the lady said, "could you please either call me Sophie, which would be quite all right, or Lady Sophie, or your ladyship, if you must, but don't call me 'lady.' Because it's just . . . uncouth." She turned at the door. The random search was over. Her voice was cold. "Besides, those bars are crammed with sugar and additives. They market them as health food, but seriously, have you read the label?"

AFTER HUNGER, OR rather, with hunger, came the boredom. Marcella had a radio in her room, but she did not dare play it; she hoped Joshua had forgotten her, she did not want to remind him she was there. The eye must have some relief from the white wall, from the yellowish veneer of the chest of drawers that were not drawers, from the scuff mark where last Filipina had dragged her suitcase across the paintwork. She had a copy of the *Evening Standard,* three days old. She read it and read it. She thought of The Lady, of the room over Cheep Cheep chicken, of the hot breath of her compatriots when they gathered, the garlic and ginger: of the green crosses, red circles, and stars of blue ink. She read the situations on offer but she did not understand the jobs. Dry liner. What is that? Perhaps she could do it?

Then after the boredom and the *Evening Standard,* the need to pass water. She had a plastic flower vase, and when it was half-full she stood on the chair, balancing it carefully, and opened the attic window. If someone were on the roof, she thought, let us say it is a bird or a man mending the guttering, let us say it is a seagull far from the sea: it will watch a thin yellow hand appear, sliding round the frame; it will see a cautious tilt of the vessel, then the thin stream running down the slates.

Once she had relieved herself in this way, she sat down on her chair and allowed herself to sip from the tumbler of water that, by sheer good fortune, had stood by her bedside when the siege began. It was cloudy, and a small fly or midge had fallen into it, and when she dabbed at it with her finger it dipped beneath the surface, evading her. Finally she trapped it against the side of the glass. She tried to lift it out, but it simply smeared itself, dark and liquid like a spot of blood. Its filthy insect essence was now in the water, but she drank it anyway, allowing six sips. She hoped that before she was sick with hunger, before her bowels became insistent, Joshua would

THE ASSASSINATION OF MARGARET THATCHER

roll out of the house, like a conqueror leaving a blighted nation behind him, and simply go back to his friends in Wiltshire, where he would boast of how he had out-smarted his parents and smashed the help with his arm so she fell and banged her head.

But this did not occur. In the late afternoon, Joshua came up the stairs and knocked at her door.

"I THOUGHT HE might be too sick," she told Mr. Mad-dox the butler. "Or too lazy, or else simply forgetful of me. But he was not any of those things, he was at the door. I knew that the bolt would not hold him for long. Though I am bound to say, he did not try at once to force entry."

Ever since she had said the word "rape," the butler had been attentive. Now, she closed her eyes, leaning against the wall of the panic room, and she could hear his impa-tience; he wanted the rest of her story. "Could you not have called for help?" he asked her.

She shook her head. The street was packed with houses, but who in Notting Hill would hear one lonely female voice from an attic window? Besides, what sort of help would she have called for? "I was not," she deployed the word carefully, "a casualty. No one had shot me. I had gone into my room to panic."

The butler said, "Come, Marcella, you can confide in me. Why do you not call me Desmond?"

"Because it would not be respectful," she said.

"No," he said. "I am not asking you for your reason, I am making you an invitation. You may use my Christian name." He took pity on her. "I see your School of English was not as good as you imagine. You do not understand some very obvious things. Common idioms have escaped you. But I was wrong to fault you when you did not know the word 'casualty.' Once it was familiar to all, being the hospital corridor where injured parties were patched together after waiting some hours. Now it is called A&E."

"I know A&E. Joshua is always took there."

"Watch your grammar," the butler said sympathetically. "You should say, 'Joshua is always taken.'"

When he issued this correction, Desmond stretched out his arm, placed his hand against the wall: as if he were holding life at bay, till the story was finished. She was not prejudiced, but she could not help the feeling that being so black his hand would leave a mark: his fingerprints. He said, "Tell your story, Marcella. It is late afternoon, to recap. You are in Notting Hill in your attic accommodation. You are hungry and have not slept well. You are in a state of agitation. You have failed to call for help, not knowing what you should call. Now it is too late. Joshua is pounding at the door. You have reason to believe, since you accuse him of snivelling, that he cherishes resentment against you. Once already he has abused you, smashing with his forearm. And now?"

"And now nothing," she said.

"No, Marcella," Mr. Maddox said. "Please trust me," and he patted his upper ribs, "secrecy resides herein. But I do not believe that he went quietly down the stairs again. That is not how this kind of story ends."

THE KNOCK AT the door was only, she knew, the boy's way of laughing at her. "Sir," she had called, "the bolt is on. I am having some private time."

"I think you are eating vermin bars," Joshua said. "Come out. You can come down and get some proper food. I need you to clean the house."

But even as he said it he was rattling the bolt. It gave as soon as he kicked it. He stood on the threshold.

"What are you hearing?" she said. "From the parents? Ski trip, they are enjoying?"

Even to herself she sounded desperate. Not one of those enquiries would have passed muster at the School of English.

"You made me break the door," Joshua said. "It will come out of your wages."

"No," Marcella said. "Your parents will never believe I kicked it in myself."

"I'll say I did it." Once again Joshua did not have his handkerchief, and rubbed his sleeve under his nose. "I'll say I had to break in, because you were having a party in here. Black men with drugs. Needles, I'll say. I'll tell them they broke the whole house up, your friends."

"What do you want?" Marcella asked. "You have my life savings already."

"What?" he said.

"You have my bag."

"What do I want with your scabby bag?"

"Fifty pounds," she said. "Inside. Please."

He laughed. "Listen," he said, "I have fifty pounds and it's gone," he snapped his fingers, "like that. Coupla pizzas. Twelve pack lager. Gone."

"But to me it is everything."

"Oh my bleeding heart!" He clutched the legend "69": he was wearing yesterday's clothes. "Forgive me if I throw up."

"Do not do that," she said," her voice low. "If you do that you have to clear it up yourself."

"Listen how it talks to me!" he said. He seemed outraged. As if it were she who were at fault for the events of the last twenty-four hours. "A person should count its blessings," he said. He was mimicking her voice.

"Let me go down," she said. "Let me past you, Joshua. I will make you eggy bread. I will get steak from the freezer, as much as you like, and you can have sausages. I will personally buy them. I will make you chips."

Hunger like a rapture: she felt light-headed. "Why do you want to starve me? And keep me here when I am willing to clean for you?"

"You people, Marcella . . ." He lingered over her name, as if he were wiping his feet on it. "You are so full of crap, and it makes me so fucking annoyed."

"I will make you chocolate milk. I will not tell anyone."

"Always going about, dusting. Dragging fucking soapy buckets up and down the stairs. It makes me puke." His eyes roamed around the room. They did not seem to focus well. "Where's your bed?"

"In that cupboard."

"What?" he said. "That's never even a cupboard, it's drawers."

Let him look for himself, Marcella thought. His eye fell on her bedding, folded in the corner. He began to believe her. "Show me," he said. Then, because he could not wait a moment to shout out his purpose, he yelled, "I'm going to rape you."

"No," she said, "you are not."

Joshua slammed shut the door. One long stride brought him to the center of the room. "Be a man, you told me. You know you did, if you say you didn't you're a fucking liar."

Unless she flew through the skylight, there was no exit. She made her calculations as to what she would do. Joshua began by kicking the chest that housed the bed, then wrenched at what he believed was a drawer. The front panel fell away, as it was designed to do. For a moment he looked dismayed: as if he did not know his own strength. He peered at the springs of the bed, its underside exposed. His brow furrowed. Inside the chest the foam mattress was folded tight, like a person in a lift doubled by stomach cramps. He pawed at the mattress. The cabinet on its castors squeaked away from him. He lashed out at it. "Ow!" He sucked his knuckles, and she felt the pain deep in her chest.

"I don't need any crap bed in a cupboard," he yelled. "I can do it to you against the wall. Don't try shouting."

"I will not shout," she said.

He stared at her. "Are you stupid? You have to shout. Did you hear what I'm going to do?"

"Yes, sir," she said, "but you cannot. Because rape is forcible violation, it is fighting back. I am not going to fight you, because I am starved and weak, and even if I were not, you are able to overcome me. So I will not take the risk to get hurt and go to the A&E. You need not rip off my clothes because I have no money for more. If you like I will take them off myself, or if you are in a hurry I can just lift up my skirt. Then you can do the thing to me, if you know how. It is not like porno, where the woman is always open. It takes time. It is difficult. It is like getting the bed out of the cupboard."

WHEN, STANDING IN the panic room, he had heard her story to the end, the butler said, "In truth, though I blame the boy, you are partly to blame."

"How is that?" Marcella asked.

"I believe you know how. You taunted him. With chocolate milk. Chips. Chocolate raisins. Implying his position was that of helpless child."

"And he wished to show himself a man," Marcella

said. "And if you call it taunting, I do not. For I know of old, if the raisins were not in his bag when he got back to school, he was ringing from Wiltshire and playing merry hell. Frankly I do not wish to live in a world where a woman cannot offer a child a meal without he feels free to concuss her."

"We cannot choose what world we live in," Desmond Maddox said. "Though we can perhaps choose our School of English. Snivel, sniffle: there is a difference."

"I myself was accused of having cereal bars. This was unjust. But I did not create mayhem."

"I have one question," the butler said. "How did you get references? From Sir Mike? You did not steal their headed letter-paper, did you?"

Marcella was inspecting the snacks in the panic room cupboard. Holding up a little packet she said, "This one is out of its sell-by date."

"Oh, nuts," Desmond said. "It will be okay. Or you can take them if you want."

"Mouldy, maybe," she said. "I will take the risk," She slipped the packet into her bag. It was her old bag, though without her life savings. When she came home from ski trip, Lady Sophie had found it tossed into the garden. "I knew it could only be yours," she said, when she handed it back.

"Once we had a chef who forged his reference," Desmond said. "He was given the quick-march. Such things are always found out."

"I cannot guess at his story," she said. "I do not think it happened to him, what happened to me."

"In fact," Desmond said, "I am moving on myself soon. Down the road, Regents Park. To work behind a Nash façade, I should say it is every butler's dream. So you will be coming to St. John's Wood, Marcella, just as I am going hence."

"Ah," she said. "Just as we had come on first-name terms. Who knows, our friendship might have blossomed. You have given notice already?"

"Not yet, so hush."

She touched her breast. "Secrecy resides herein."

"I found the post in The Lady," he said. "Nice family. Never come into this country more than one, two, three weeks a year. Bring their entourage with their own chef, they don't eat English food on grounds of taste and hygiene and because poison might get in it. So it's cushy number. Security guarding, really, nine-ten months of the year."

Desmond had taken his hand from the wall. Her eyes searched and searched for a mark but she could not see one. Still she searched; she did not want to be faulted for carelessness, in her first week. She asked, "Your new family, do they have a panic room?"

"Beneath those houses," the butler said, "you should see what goes on. No one suspects the half of it. The whole earth is dug out. Spaciousness beneath. The panic room is seven times the size of this one. The whole of London can fall down around them and yet their freezer is fully stocked. All showers are multi-jet steam cabinets, plus the kitchen has coffee machine built in, ice machine, temperature-controlled cabinet for wine storage, sous vide machine with vacuum sealer, and an air-filtration system that is suitable for allergy sufferers. The walls are built to withstand a nucular bomb."

"Nuclear," she said.

She saw the look that flitted across his face: don't you correct my English, yellow bitch. At once it was replaced by a look of bored neutrality, as he led her from the panic room and up the stairs. But she had seen it; she would not forget it; she did not forget things, except that she had forgotten those events that followed the first blow. There was an area of darkness, a darkness that flowed like a river, a darkness that pooled like a lake; then after some time, how long she could not know, there was bright light, and voices and pain. When she opened her eyes, the first thing she saw was the puzzled, anxious face of the child Jonquil, who dabbed at her mouth with a tissue held in her small fingers. She realized that, in default of her own bed, Joshua had used his sister's for her violation, but she recalled nothing of that; the bruises were fresh on her back where he had dragged her down the stairs, but she did not feel it at the time. The stencilled sheep on the headboard said yes sir, no sir, three bags full; the calves sank to their knees in the lush meadow grass; the bluebirds shivered on their wires as the mobile chimed in the breeze.

* * *

IN SUBSEQUENT DAYS, after Desmond had said his farewells and she had settled into her new situation, she thought of the butler and his new employers at Regents Park, and wondered how they were all getting on. If they came just once, twice, three times a year, they might never visit the panic room. But if the need should arise, and they found themselves below ground: what would they do when the first panic ebbed, when it subsided into that dull state of fear in which so many of us live our lives, once we leave our native shores, our parents' house? How would they pass the weeks, while London crumbled and the feral dogs scavenged in the streets, while the air filters clogged and the freezer's stocks were depleted? Would they have books to read? Would they complete puzzles? Would they play games? She imagined solemn gentlemen from the Middle East, white robes hoisted to show hairy legs and black silk socks; she imagined their black-swathed wives, hands emerging to clutch hands, each finger weighted with jewels. Here we go round the mulberry bush. Ring of roses. She remembered the newspaper, the *Evening Standard*, that had sustained her during those lost hours in Notting Hill. The situations she could have had. "Work waiting," the adverts said. "Operative wanted for confined spaces."

Work is always waiting, you cannot escape it. Dry liners and fitters were needed, trackmen, jointers and underpinners, multitrade operators and plastering gangs. When she got out of hospital, and was ready to work again, she had visited an agency. She mentioned these trades and confessed she did not know what they were. They advised playing to the strengths listed in her letter of recommendation: *Marcella is always willing*. "However," they said to her, "your cosmetic impression is bad."

She did not deny it. She had lost teeth in the attack. But we all lose them, sooner or later. She had said this to the woman at the agency: who then agreed to keep her CV on file. A week went by, and nothing, despite ringing them every day.

Every day she looked at the *Standard*. Welders were wanted, painters and fabricators. The word snagged her attention: fabricators. She had turned as usual to the columns of The Lady, and there she found her current post in St. John's Wood. When she was called for her interview, a friend went for her, one with more teeth; and when she presented herself on her first day, no one had said, you are not the woman we saw last week. Desmond had simply told her, "I am Mr. Maddox, the butler"; his glance had passed over her; he gave her an overall, showed her over the house, and allowed her to visit the panic room, the first she had ever seen.

Sometimes, in St. John's Wood, she has dreams about her previous job and how it ended: in a hot exchange of words, in the banging of the cabinet-bed across the floor: in blackout, in absence. She is no longer sure that the facts were exactly those she had given to the butler. It may be she has been a fabricator. That some painting has occurred, or underpinning. Time has passed. It is a great healer or so they aver. Perhaps the pain she felt was heartbreak, not knuckles. Perhaps the story did not happen to her, but to her friend; women work for each other's wages, names are erased and histories pooled, and you cannot tell these friends apart, when they are rolled in their blankets, only heads visible and eyes closed, lying in the miasma of chicken fat and frying oil. The boy will be punished. He will say he does not understand why. The camera will catch him on the steps of the law court, a burger in his hand, his mouth open in anticipation. Contested versions of conversations will be aired. (Snivel, sniffle.) The issue of consent will be raised; when did she give hers? Was it when she left her country? Was it when she took the job? Was it when she agreed to be born? The case will collapse for lack of evidence. Money will change hands. Here in S.t John's Wood she will be safe, or not. She dreams of awakening, and it is only the dream that makes her think, this happened to Marcella, no one else; she sees the Alpine sunlight sharp as glass, and the child Jonquil, back from ski break, sniffling as she dabs the blood from her face.

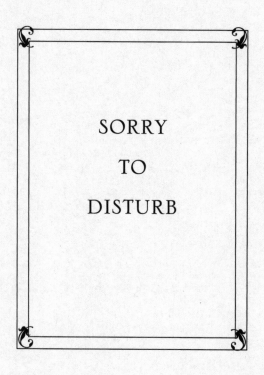

SORRY

TO

DISTURB

In those days, the doorbell didn't ring often, and if it did I would draw back into the body of the house. Only at a persistent ring would I creep over the carpets, and make my way to the front door with its spy hole. We were big on bolts and shutters, deadlocks and mortises, safety chains and windows that were high and barred. Through the spy hole I saw a distraught man in a crumpled, silver-gray suit: thirties, Asian. He had dropped back from the door, and was looking about him, at the closed and locked door opposite, and up the dusty marble stairs. He patted his pockets, took out a balled-up handkerchief, and rubbed it across his face. He looked so fraught that his sweat could have been tears. I opened the door.

At once he raised his hands as if to show he was unarmed, his handkerchief dropping like a white flag. "Madam!" Ghastly pale I must have looked, under the light that dappled the tiled walls with swinging shadows. But then he took a breath, tugged at his creased jacket, ran a hand through his hair and conjured up his business card. "Muhammad Ijaz. Import-Export. I am so sorry to disturb your afternoon. I am totally lost. Would you permit use of your telephone?"

I stood aside to let him in. No doubt I smiled. Given what would ensue, I must suppose I did. "Of course. If it's working today."

I walked ahead and he followed, talking; an important deal, he had almost closed it, visit to client in person necessary, time—he worked up his sleeve and consulted a fake Rolex—time running out; he had the address— again he patted his pockets—but the office is not where it should be. He spoke into the telephone in rapid Arabic, fluent, aggressive, his eyebrows shooting up, finally shaking his head; he put down the receiver, looked at it in regret; then up at me, with a sour smile. Weak mouth, I thought. Almost a handsome man, but not: slim, sallow, easily thrown. "I am in your debt, madam," he said. "Now I must dash."

I wanted to offer him a what—bathroom break? Comfort stop? I had no idea how to phrase it. The absurd phrase *wash and brushup* came into my mind. But he was already heading for the door—though from the way the call had concluded I thought they might not be so keen to see him, at his destination, as he was to see them. "This crazy city," he said. "They are always digging up the streets and moving them. I am so sorry to break in on your privacy." In the hall, he darted another glance around and up the stairs. "Only the British will ever help you." He skidded across the hall and prized open the outer door with its heavy ironwork screen; admitting, for a moment, the dull roar of traffic from Medina Road. The door swung back, he was gone. I closed the hall door discreetly, and melted into the oppressive hush. The air conditioner rattled away, like an old relative with a loose cough. The air was heavy with insecticide; sometimes I sprayed it as I walked, and it fell about me like bright mists, veils. I resumed my phrasebook and tape, Fifth Lesson: *I'm living in Jeddah. I'm busy today. God give you strength!*

When my husband came home in the afternoon I told him: "A lost man was here. Pakistani. Businessman. I let him in to phone."

My husband was silent. The air conditioner hacked away. He walked into the shower, having evicted the cockroaches. Walked out again, dripping, naked, lay on the bed, stared at the ceiling. Next day I swept the business card into a bin.

In the afternoon the doorbell rang again. Ijaz had come back, to apologize, to explain, to thank me for rescuing him. I made him some instant coffee and he sat down and told me about himself.

IT WAS THEN June 1983. I had been in Saudi Arabia for six months. My husband worked for a Toronto-based company of consulting geologists, and had been seconded by them to the Ministry of Mineral Resources. Most of his colleagues were housed in family "compounds" of various sizes, but the single men and a childless couple like ourselves had to take what they could get. This was our second flat. The American bachelor who had occupied it before had been moved out in haste. Upstairs, in this block of four flats, lived a Saudi civil servant with his wife and baby; the fourth flat was empty; on the ground floor across the hall from us lived a Pakistani accountant who worked for a government minister, handling his personal finances. Meeting the womenfolk in the hall or on the stairs—one blacked-out head to toe, one partly veiled— the bachelor had livened up their lives by calling "Hello!" Or possibly "Hi there!"

There was no suggestion of further impertinence. But a complaint had been made, and he vanished, and we went to live there instead. The flat was small by Saudi standards. It had beige carpet and off-white wallpaper on which there was a faint crinkled pattern, almost indiscernible. The windows were guarded by heavy wooden shutters that you cranked down by turning a handle on the inside. Even with the shutters up it was dim and I needed the strip lights on all day. The rooms were closed off from each other by double doors of dark wood, heavy like coffin lids. It was like living in a funeral home, with samples stacked around you, and insect opportunists frying themselves on the lights.

HE WAS A graduate of a Miami business school, Ijaz said, and his business, his main business just now, was bottled water. Had the deal gone through, yesterday? He was evasive—obviously, there was nothing simple about it. He waved a hand—give it time, give it time.

I had no friends in this city as yet. Social life, such as it was, centered on private houses; there were no cinemas, theaters or lecture halls. There were sports grounds, but women could not attend them. No "mixed gatherings" were allowed. The Saudis did not mix with foreign workers. They looked down on them as necessary evils, though white-skinned, English-speaking expatriates were at the top of the pecking order. Others—Ijaz, for example—

were "Third Country Nationals," a label that exposed them to every kind of truculence, insult and daily complication. Indians and Pakistanis staffed the shops and small businesses. Filipinos worked on building sites. Men from Thailand cleaned the streets. Bearded Yemenis sat on the pavement outside lock-up shops, their skirts rucked up, their hairy legs thrust out, their flip-flops inches from the whizzing cars.

I am married, Ijaz said, and to an American; you must meet her. Maybe, he said, maybe you could do something for her, you know? What I foresaw at best was the usual Jeddah arrangement, of couples shackled together. Women had no motive power in this city; they had no driving licenses, and only the rich had drivers. So couples who wanted to visit must do it together. I didn't think Ijaz and my husband would be friends. Ijaz was too restless and nervy. He laughed at nothing. He was always twitching his collar and twisting his feet in their scuffed Oxfords, always tapping the fake Rolex, always apologizing. Our apartment is down by the port, he said, with my sister-in-law and my brother, but he's back in Miami just now, and my mother's here just now for a visit, and my wife from America, and my son and my daughter, aged six, aged eight. He reached for his wallet and showed me a strange-looking, steeple-headed little boy. "Saleem."

When he left, he thanked me again for trusting him to come into my house. Why, he said, he might have been anybody. But it is not the British way to think badly of needy strangers. At the door he shook my hand. That's that, I thought. Part of me thought, it had better be.

FOR ONE WAS always observed: overlooked, without precisely being seen, recognized. My Pakistani neighbor Yasmin, to get between my flat and hers, would fling a scarf over her rippling hair, then peep around the door; with nervous, pecking movements she hopped across the marble, head swiveling from side to side, in case someone should choose that very moment to shoulder through the heavy street door. Sometimes, irritated by the dust that blew under the door and banked up on the marble, I would go out into the hall with a long broom. My male Saudi neighbor would come down from the first floor on his way out to his car and step over my brushstrokes without looking at me, his head averted. He was according me invisibility, as a mark of respect to another man's wife.

I was not sure that Ijaz accorded me this respect. Our situation was anomalous and ripe for misunderstanding: I had an afternoon caller. He probably thought that only the kind of woman who took a lot of risks with herself would let a stranger into her house. Yet I could not guess what he probably thought. Surely a Miami business school, surely his time in the West, had made my attitude seem more normal than not? His talk was relaxed now he knew me, full of feeble jokes that he laughed at himself; but then there was the jiggling of his foot, the pulling of his collar, the tapping of his fingers. I had noticed, listening to my tape, that his situation was anticipated in the Nineteenth Lesson: *I gave the address to my driver, but when we arrived, there wasn't any house at this address.* I hoped to show by my brisk friendliness what was only the truth, that our situation could be simple, because I felt no attraction to him at all; so little that I felt apologetic about it. That is where it began to go wrong—my feeling that I must bear out the national character he had given me, and that I must not slight him or refuse a friendship, in case he thought it was because he was a Third Country National.

For his second visit, and his third, were an interruption, almost an irritation. Having no choice in that city, I had decided to cherish my isolation, coddle it. I was ill in those days, and subject to a fierce drug regime that gave me blinding headaches, made me slightly deaf and made me, though I was hungry, unable to eat. The drugs were expensive and had to be imported from England; my husband's company brought them in by courier. Word of this leaked out, and the company wives decided I was taking fertility drugs; but I did not know this, and my ignorance made our conversations peculiar and, to me, slightly menacing. Why were they always talking, on the occasions of forced company sociability, about women who'd had miscarriages but now had a bouncing babe in the buggy? An older woman confided that her two were adopted; I looked at them and thought Jesus, where from, the zoo? My Pakistani neighbour also joined in the cooing over the offspring that I would have shortly—she was in on the rumors, but I put her hints down to the fact that she was carrying her first child and wanted company. I saw her most mornings for an interval of coffee and chat, and I would rather steer her to talking about Islam, which was easy enough; she was an educated woman and keen to instruct. June 6th: "Spent two hours with my neighbor," says my diary, "widening the cultural gap."

Next day, my husband brought home air tickets and my exit visa for our first home leave, which was seven weeks away. Thursday, June 9th: "Found a white hair in my head." At home there was a general election, and we sat up through the night to listen to the results on the BBC World Service. When we turned out the light, the grocer's daughter jigged through my dreams to the strains of "Lillibulero." Friday was a holiday, and we slept undisturbed till the noon prayer call. Ramadan began. Wednesday, June 15th: "Read *The Twyborn Affair* and vomited sporadically."

On the sixteenth our neighbors across the hall left for pilgrimage, robed in white. They rang our doorbell before they left: "Is there anything we can bring you from Mecca?" June 19th saw me desperate for change, moving the furniture around the sitting room and recording "not much improvement." I write that I am prey to "unpleasant and intrusive thoughts," but I do not say what they are. I describe myself as "hot, sick and morose." By July 4th I must have been happier, because I listened to the *Eroica* while doing the ironing. But on the morning of July 10th, I got up first, put the coffee on, and went into the sitting room to find that the furniture had been trying to move itself back. An armchair was leaning to the left, as if executing some tipsy dance; at one side its base rested on the carpet, but the other side was a foot in the air, and balanced finely on the rim of a flimsy wastepaper basket. Open-mouthed, I shot back into the bedroom; it was the Eid holiday, and my husband was still half awake. I gibbered at him. Silent, he rose, put on his glasses, and followed me. He stood in the doorway of the sitting room. He looked around and told me without hesitation it had nothing to do with him. He walked into the bathroom. I heard him close the door, curse the cockroaches, switch on the shower. I said later, I must be walking in my sleep. Do you think that's it? Do you think I did it? July 12th: "Execution dream again."

The trouble was, Ijaz knew I was at home; how would I be going anywhere? One afternoon I left him standing in the hall, while he pressed and pressed the doorbell, and next time, when I let him in, he asked me where I had been; when I said, "Ah, sorry, I must have been with my neighbor," I could see he did not believe me, and he looked at me so sorrowfully that my heart went out to him. Jeddah fretted him, it galled him, and he missed, he said, America, he missed his visits to London, he must go soon, take a break; when was our leave, perhaps we might meet up? I explained I did not live in London, which surprised him; he seemed to suspect it was an evasion, like my failure to answer the door. "Because I could get an exit visa," he said again. "Meet up there. Without all this . . ." he gestured at the coffin-lid doors, the heavy, willful furniture.

He made me laugh that day, telling me about his first girlfriend, his American girlfriend whose nickname was Patches. It was easy to picture her, sassy and suntanned, astonishing him one day by pulling off her top, bouncing her bare breasts at him and putting an end to his wan virginity. The fear he felt, the terror of touching her . . . his shameful performance . . . recalling it, he knuckled his forehead. I was charmed, I suppose. How often does a man tell you these things? I told my husband, hoping to make him laugh, but he didn't. Often, to be helpful, I hoovered up the cockroaches before his return from the Ministry. He shed his clothes and headed off. I heard the splash of the shower. Nineteenth Lesson: *Are you married? Yes, my wife is with me, she's standing there in the corner of the room.* I imagined the cockroaches, dark and flailing in the dust bag.

I went back to the dining table, on which I was writing a comic novel. It was a secret activity I never mentioned to the company wives, and barely mentioned to myself. I scribbled under the strip light, until it was time to drive out for food shopping. You had to shop between sunset prayers and night prayers; if you mistimed it, then at the first prayer call the shops slammed down their shutters, trapping you inside, or outside in the wet heat of the car park. The malls were patrolled by volunteers from the Committee for the Propagation of Virtue and the Elimination of Vice.

At the end of July Ijaz brought his family for tea. Mary-Beth was a small woman but seemed swollen beneath the skin; spiritless, freckled, limp, she was a faded redhead who seemed huddled into herself, unused to conversation. A silent daughter with eyes like dark stars had been trussed up for the visit in a frilly white dress. At six, steeple-headed Saleem had lost his baby fat, and his movements were tentative, as if his limbs were snappable. His eyes were watchful; Mary-Beth hardly met my gaze at all. What had Ijaz told her? That he was taking her to see a woman who was something like he'd like her to be? It was an unhappy afternoon. I can only have got through it because I was buoyed by an uprush of anticipation; my bags were packed for our flight home. A day earlier, when I had gone into the spare room where I kept my clothes, I had met another dismaying sight. The doors of the fitted wardrobe, which were large and solid like the other coffin lids, had been removed from their hinges; they had been replaced, but hung by the lower hinges only, so that their upper halves flapped like the wings of some ramshackle flying machine.

On August 1st we left King Abdulaziz International Airport in an electrical storm, and had a bumpy flight. I was curious about Mary-Beth's situation and hoped to see her again, though another part of me hoped that she and Ijaz would simply vanish.

I DIDN'T RETURN to Jeddah till the very end of November, having left my book with an agent. Just before our leave I had met my Saudi neighbor, a young mother taking a part-time literature course at the women's university. Education for women was regarded as a luxury, an ornament, a way for a husband to boast of his broadmindedness; Munira couldn't even begin to do her assignments, and I took to going up to her flat in the late mornings and doing them for her, while she sat on the floor in her négligée, watching Egyptian soaps on TV and eating sunflower seeds. We three women, Yasmin and Munira and

I, had become midmorning friends; all the better for them to watch me, I thought, and discuss me when I'm gone. It was easier for Yasmin and me to go upstairs, because to come down Munira had to get kitted out in full veil and abaya; again, that treacherous, hovering moment on the public territory of the staircase, where a man might burst through from the street and shout "Hi!" Yasmin was a delicate woman, like a princess in a Persian miniature; younger than myself, she was impeccably soignée, finished with a flawless glaze of good manners and restraint. Munira was nineteen, with coarse, eager good looks, a pale skin, and a mane of hair that crackled with static and seemed to lead a vital, separate life; her laugh was a raucous cackle. She and Yasmin sat on cushions but gave me a chair; they insisted. They served Nescafé in my honor, though I would have preferred a sludgy local brew. I had learned the crude effectiveness of caffeine against migraine; some nights, sleepless, pacing, I careened off the walls, and only the dawn prayer call sent me to bed, still thinking furiously of books I might write.

Ijaz rang the doorbell on December 6th. He was so

very pleased to see me after my long leave; beaming, he said, "Now you are more like Patches than ever." I felt a flare of alarm; nothing, nothing had been said about this before. I was slimmer, he said, and looked well—my prescription drugs had been cut down, and I had been exposed to some daylight, I supposed that was what was doing it. But, "No, there is something different about you," he said. One of the company wives had said the same. She thought, no doubt, that I had conceived my baby at last.

I led Ijaz into the sitting room, while he trailed me with compliments, and made the coffee. "Maybe it's my book," I said, sitting down. "You see, I've written a book . . ." My voice tailed off. This was not his world. No one read books in Jeddah. You could buy anything in the shops except alcohol or a bookcase. My neighbor Yasmin, though she was an English graduate, said she had never read a book since her marriage; she was too busy making supper parties every night. I have had a little success, I explained, or I hope for a little success, I have written a novel you see, and an agent has taken it on.

"It is a storybook? For children?"

"For adults."

"You did this during your vacation?"

"No, I was always writing it." I felt deceitful. I was writing it when I didn't answer the doorbell.

"Your husband will pay to have it published for you."

"No, with luck someone will pay me. A publisher. The agent hopes he can sell it."

"This agent, where did you meet him?"

I could hardly say, in the *Writers' & Artists' Yearbook.* "In London. At his office."

"But you do not live in London," Ijaz said, as if laying down an ace. He was out to find something wrong with my story. "Probably he is no good. He may steal your money."

I saw of course that in his world, the term *agent* would cover some broad, unsavory categories. But what about "Import-Export," as written on his business cards? That didn't sound to me like the essence of probity. I wanted to argue; I was still upset about Patches; without warning, Ijaz seemed to have changed the terms of engagement between us. "I don't think so. I haven't given him money. His firm, it's well known." Their office is where? Ijaz sniffed, and I pressed on, trying to make my case; though why did I think that an office in William IV Street was a guarantee of moral worth? Ijaz knew London well. "Charing Cross tube?" He still looked affronted. "Near Trafalgar Square?"

Ijaz grunted. "You went to this premises alone?"

I couldn't placate him. I gave him a biscuit. I didn't expect him to understand what I was up to, but he seemed aggrieved that another man had entered my life. "How is Mary-Beth?" I asked.

"She has some kidney disease."

I was shocked. "Is it serious?"

He raised his shoulders; not a shrug, more a rotation of the joints, as if easing some old ache. "She must go back to America for treatment. It's okay. I'm getting rid of her anyway."

I looked away. I hadn't imagined this. "I'm sorry you're unhappy."

"You see really I don't know what's the matter with her," he said testily. "She is always miserable and moping."

"You know, this is not the easiest place for a woman to live."

But did he know? Irritated, he said, "She wanted a big car. So I got a big car. What more does she want me to do?"

December 6th: "Ijaz stayed too long," the diary says. Next day he was back. After the way he had spoken of his wife—and the way he had compared me to dear old Patches from his Miami days—I didn't think I should see him again. But he had hatched a scheme and he wasn't going to let it go. I should come to a dinner party with my husband and meet his family and some of his business contacts. He had been talking about this project before my leave and I knew he set great store by it. I wanted, if I could, to do him some good; he would appear to his customers to be more a man of the world if he could arrange an international gathering, if—let's be blunt—he could produce some white friends. Now the time had come. His sister-in-law was already cooking, he said. I wanted to meet her; I admired these diaspora Asians, their polyglot enterprise, the way they withstood rebuffs, and I wanted to see if she was more Western or Eastern or what. "We have to arrange the transportation," Ijaz said. "I shall come Thursday, when your husband is here. Four o'clock. To give him directions." I nodded. No use drawing a map. They might move the streets again.

The meeting of December 8th was not a success. Ijaz was late, but didn't seem to know it. My husband dispensed the briefest host's courtesies, then sat down firmly in his armchair, which was the one that had tried to levitate. He seemed, by his watchful silence, ready to put an end to any nonsense, from furniture or guests or any other quarter. Sitting on the edge of the sofa, Ijaz flaked his baklava over his lap, he juggled with his fork and jiggled his coffee cup. After our dinner party, he said, almost the next day, he was flying to America on business. "I shall route via London. Just for some recreation. Just to relax, three–four days."

My husband must have stirred himself to ask if he had friends there. "Very old friend," Ijaz said, brushing crumbs to the carpet. "Living at Trafalgar Square. A good district. You know it?"

My heart sank; it was a physical feeling, of the months falling away from me, months in which I'd had little natural light. When Ijaz left—and he kept hovering on the threshold, giving further and better street directions—I didn't know what to say, so I went into the bathroom, kicked out the cockroaches and cowered under the stream of tepid water. Wrapped in a towel, I lay on the bed in the dark. I could hear my husband—I hoped it was he, and not the armchair—moving around in the sitting room. Sometimes in those days when I closed my eyes I felt that I was looking back into my own skull. I could see the hemispheres of my brain. They were convoluted and the color of putty.

THE FAMILY APARTMENT down by the port was filled with cooking smells and crammed with furniture. There were photographs on every surface, carpets laid on carpets. It was a hot night, and the air conditioners labored and hacked, spitting out water, coughing up lungfuls of mold spores, blights. The table linen was limp and heavily fringed, and I kept fingering these fringes, which felt like nylon fur, like the ears of a teddy bear; they comforted me, though I felt electric with tension. At the table a vast lumpen elder presided, a woman with a long chomping jaw; she was like Quentin Matsys's Ugly Duchess, except in a spangled sari. The sister-in-law was a bright, brittle woman, who gave a sarcastic lilt to all her phrases. I could see why; it was evident, from her knowing looks, that Ijaz had talked about me, and set me up in some way; if he was proposing me as his next wife, I offered little improvement on the original. Her scorn became complete when she saw I barely touched the food at my elbow; I kept smiling and nodding, demurring and deferring, nibbling a parsley leaf and sipping my Fanta. I wanted to eat, but she might as well have offered me stones on a doily. Did Ijaz think, as the Saudis did, that Western marriages meant nothing? That they were entered impulsively and on impulse broken? Did he assume my husband was as keen to offload me as he was to lose Mary-Beth? From his point of view the evening was not going well. He had expected two supermarket managers, he told us, important men with spending power; now night prayers were over, the traffic was on the move again, all down Palestine Road and along the Corniche the traffic lights were turning green, from Thumb Street to the Pepsi flyover the city was humming, but where were they? Sweat dripped from his face. Fingers jabbed the buttons of the telephone. "Okay, he is delayed? He has left? He is coming now?" He rapped down the receiver, then gazed at the phone as if willing it to chirp back at him, like some pet fowl. "Time means nothing here," he joked, pulling at his collar. The sister-in-law shrugged and turned down her mouth. She never rested, but passed airily through the room in peach chiffon, each time returning from the kitchen with another laden tray; out of sight, presumably, some oily skivvy was weeping into the dishes. The silent elder put away a large part of the food, pulling the plates toward her and working through them systematically till the pattern showed beneath her questing fingers; you looked away, and when you looked back the plate was clean. Sometimes, the phone rang: "Okay, they're nearly here," Ijaz called. Ten minutes, and his brow furrowed again. "Maybe they're lost."

"Sure they're lost," sister-in-law sang. She sniggered; she was enjoying herself. Nineteenth Lesson, translate these sentences: *So long as he holds the map the wrong way up, he will never find the house. They started traveling this morning, but have still not arrived.* It seemed a hopeless business, trying to get anywhere, and the textbook confessed it. I was not really learning Arabic, of course, I was too impatient; I was leafing through the lessons, looking for phrases that might be useful if I could say them. We stayed long, long into the evening, waiting for the men who had never intended to come; in the end, wounded and surly, Ijaz escorted us to the door. I heard my husband take in a breath of wet air. "We'll never have to do it again," I consoled him. In the car, "You have to feel for him," I said. No answer.

December 13th: My diary records that I am oppressed by "the darkness, the ironing and the smell of drains." I could no longer play my *Eroica* tape as it had twisted itself up in the innards of the machine. In my idle moments I had summarized forty chapters of *Oliver Twist* for the use of my upstairs neighbor. Three days later I was "horribly unstable and restless," and reading the *Lyttelton/Hart-Davis Letters*. Later that week I was cooking with my neighbor

Yasmin. I recorded "an afternoon of graying pain." All the same, Ijaz was out of the country and I realized I breathed easier when I was not anticipating the ring of the door-bell. December 16th, I was reading *The Philosopher's Pupil* and visiting my own student upstairs. Munira took my forty chapter summaries, flicked through them, yawned, and switched on the TV. "What is a workhouse?" I tried to explain about the English poor law, but her expression glazed; she had never heard of poverty. She yelled out for her servant, an ear-splitting yell, and the girl—a beaten-down Indonesian—brought in Munira's daughter for my diversion. A heavy, solemn child, she was beginning to walk, or stamp, under her own power, her hands flailing for a hold on the furniture. She would fall on her bottom with a grunt, haul herself up again by clutching the sofa; the cushions slid away from her, she tumbled backward, banged on the floor her large head with its corkscrew curls, and lay there wailing. Munira laughed at her: "White nigger, isn't it?" She didn't get her flat nose from my side, she explained. Or those fat lips either. It's my husband's people, but of course, they're blaming me.

January 2nd 1984: We went to a dark little restaurant off Khalid bin Wahlid Street, where we were seated behind a lattice screen in the "family area." In the main part of the room men were dining with each other. The business of eating out was more a gesture than a pleasure; you would gallop through the meal, because without wine and its rituals there was nothing to slow it, and the waiters, who had no concept that a man and woman might eat together for more than sustenance, prided themselves on picking up your plate as soon as you had finished and slapping down another, and rushing you back onto the dusty street. That dusty orange glare, perpetual, like the lighting of a bad sci-fi film; the constant snarl and rumble of traffic; I had become afraid of traffic accidents, which were frequent, and every time we drove out at night I saw the gaping spaces beneath bridges and flyovers; they seemed to me like amphitheaters in which the traffic's casualties enacted, flickering, their final moments. Sometimes, when I set foot outside the apartment, I started to shake. I blamed it on the drugs I was taking; the dose had been increased again. When I saw the other wives they didn't seem to be having these difficulties. They talked about paddling pools and former lives they had led in Hong Kong. They got up little souk trips to buy jewelry, so that sliding on their scrawny tanned arms their bracelets clinked and chimed, like ice cubes knocking together. On Valentine's Day we went to a cheese party; you had to imagine the wine. I was bubbling with happiness; a letter had come from William IV Street, to tell me my novel had been sold. Spearing his Edam with a cocktail stick, my husband's boss loomed over me: "Hubby tells me you're having a book published. That must be costing him a pretty penny."

Ijaz, I assumed, was still in America. After all, he had his marital affairs to sort out, as well as business. He doesn't reappear in the diary till March 17th, St. Patrick's Day, when I recorded, "Phone call, highly unwelcome." For politeness, I asked how business was; as ever, he was evasive. He had something else to tell me: "I've got rid of Mary-Beth. She's gone."

"What about the children?"

"Saleem is staying with me. The girl, it doesn't matter. She can have her if she wants."

"Ijaz, look, I must say good-bye. I hear the doorbell."
What a lie.

"Who is it?"

What, did he think I could see through the wall? For a second I was so angry I forgot there was only a phantom at the door. "Perhaps my neighbor," I said meekly.

"See you soon," Ijaz said.

I decided that night I could no longer bear it. I did not feel I could bear even one more cup of coffee together. But I had no means of putting an end to it, and for this I excused myself, saying I had been made helpless by the society around me. I was not able to bring myself to speak to Ijaz directly. I still had no power in me to snub him. But the mere thought of him made me squirm inside with shame, at my own general cluelessness, and at the sad little lies he had told to misrepresent his life, and the situation into which we had blundered; I thought of the sister-in-law, her peach chiffon and her curled lip.

Next day when my husband came home I sat him down and instigated a conversation. I asked him to write to Ijaz and ask him not to call on me anymore, as I was afraid that the neighbors had noticed his visits and might draw the wrong conclusion: which, as he knew, could be dangerous to us all. My husband heard me out. You need not write much, I pleaded, he will get the point. I should be able to sort this out for myself, but I am not allowed to, it is beyond my power, or it seems to be. I heard my own voice, jangled, grating; I was doing what I had wriggled so hard to avoid, I was sheltering behind the mores of this society, off-loading the problem I had created for myself in a way that was feminine, weak and spiteful.

My husband saw all this. Not that he spoke. He got up, took his shower. He lay in the rattling darkness, in the bedroom where the wooden shutters blocked out the merest chink of afternoon glare. I lay beside him. The evening prayer call woke me from my doze. My husband had risen to write the letter. I remember the snap of the lock as he closed it in his briefcase.

I have never asked him what he put in the letter, but whatever it was it worked. There was nothing—not a chastened note pushed under the door, nor a regretful phone call. Just silence. The diary continues but Ijaz exits from it. I read *Zuckerman Unbound*, *The Present & The Past*, and *The Bottle Factory Outing*. The company's post office box went missing, with all the incoming mail in it. You would think a post box was a fixed thing and wouldn't go wandering of its own volition, but it was many days before it was found, at a distant post office, and I suppose a post box can move if furniture can. We drifted toward our next leave. May 10th, we attended a farewell party for an escapee whose contract was up. "Fell over while dancing and sprained my ankle." May 11th: With my ankle strapped up, "watched *The Texas Chainsaw Massacre*."

I had much more time to serve in Jeddah. I didn't leave finally till the spring of 1986. By that time we had been rehoused twice more, shuttled around the city and finally outside it to a compound off the freeway. I never heard of my visitor again. The woman trapped in the flat on the corner of Al-Suror Street seems a relative stranger, and I ask myself what she should have done, how she could have managed it better. She should have thrown those drugs away, for one thing; they are nowadays a medication of last resort, because everybody knows they make you frightened, deaf and sick. But about Ijaz? She should never have opened the door in the first place. Discretion is the better part of valor; she's always said that. Even after all this time it's hard to grasp exactly what happened. I try to write it as it occurred but I find myself changing the names to protect the guilty. I wonder if Jeddah left me forever off-kilter in some way, tilted from the vertical and condemned to see life skewed. I can never be certain that doors will stay closed and on their hinges, and I do not know, when I turn out the lights at night, whether the house is quiet as I left it or the furniture is frolicking in the dark.

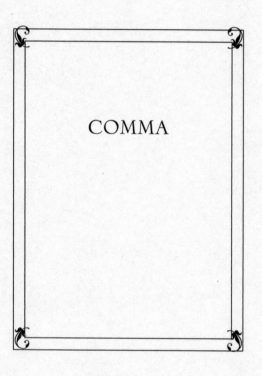

COMMA

I can see Mary Joplin now, in the bushes crouching with her knees apart, her cotton frock stretched across her thighs. In the hottest summer (and this was it) Mary had a sniffle, and she would rub the tip of her upturned nose, meditatively, with the back of her hand, and inspect the glistening snail trail that was left. We squatted, both of us, up to our ears in tickly grass: grass which, as midsummer passed, turned from tickly to scratchy and etched white lines, like the art of a primitive tribe, across our bare legs. Sometimes we would rise together, as if pulled up by invisible strings. Parting the rough grass in swathes, we would push a little closer to where we knew we were going, and where we knew we should not go. Then, as if by some predetermined signal, we would flounce down again, so we would be half-invisible if God looked over the fields.

Buried in the grass we talked: myself monosyllabic, guarded, eight years old, wearing too-small shorts of black-and-white check, that had fitted me last year; Mary with her scrawny arms, her kneecaps like saucers of bone, her bruised legs, her snigger and her cackle and her snort. Some unknown hand, her own perhaps, had placed on her rat-tails a twisted white ribbon; by afternoon it had skewed itself around to the side, so that her head looked like a badly tied parcel. Mary Joplin put questions to me: "Are you rich?"

I was startled. "I don't think so. We're about middle. Are you rich?"

She pondered. She smiled at me as if we were comrades now. "We're about middle too."

Poverty meant upturned blue eyes and a begging bowl. A charity child. You'd have colored patches sewn on your clothes. In a fairy-tale picture book you live in the forest under the dripping gables, your roof is thatch. You have a basket with a patchwork cover with which you venture out to your grandma. Your house is made of cake.

WHEN I WENT to my grandma's it was empty handed, and I was sent just to be company for her. I didn't know what this meant. Sometimes I stared at the wall till she let me go home again. Sometimes she let me pod peas. Sometimes she made me hold her wool while she wound it. She snapped at me to call me to attention if I let my wrists droop. When I said I was weary, she said I didn't know the meaning of the word. She'd show me weary, she said. She carried on muttering: weary, I'll show her who's weary, I'll weary her with a good slap.

When my wrists drooped and my attention faltered it was because I was thinking of Mary Joplin. I knew not to mention her name and the pressure of not mentioning her made her, in my imagination, beaten thin and flat, attenuated, starved away, a shadow of herself, so I was no longer sure whether she existed when I was not with her. But then next day in the morning's first dazzle, when I stood on our doorstep, I would see Mary leaning against the house opposite, smirking, scratching herself under her frock, and she would stick her tongue out at me until it was stretched to the root.

If my mother looked out she would see her too; or maybe not.

ON THOSE AFTERNOONS, buzzing, sleepy, our wandering had a veiled purpose and we drew closer and closer to the Hathaways' house. I did not call it that then, and until that summer I hadn't known it existed; it seemed it had materialized during my middle childhood, as our boundaries pushed out, as we strayed further from the village's core. Mary had found it before I did. It stood on its own, no other house built onto it, and we knew without debate that it was the house of the rich; stone-built, with one lofty round tower, it stood in its gardens bounded by a wall, but not too high a wall for us to climb: to drop softly, between the bushes on the other side. From there we saw that in the beds of this garden the roses were already scorched into heavy brown blebs on the stalk. The lawns were parched. Long windows glinted, and around the house, on the side from which we approached, there ran a veranda or loggia or terrace; I did not have a word for it, and no use asking Mary.

She said cheerily, as we wandered cross-country, "Me dad says, you're bloody daft, Mary, do you know that? He says, when they turned you out, love, they broke the bloody mold. He says, Mary, you don't know arseholes from Tuesday."

On that first day at the Hathaways' house, sheltered in the depth of the bushes, we waited for the rich to come out of the glinting windows that were also doors; we waited to see what actions they would perform. Mary Joplin whispered to me, "Your mam dun't know where you are."

"Well, your mam neither."

As the afternoon wore on, Mary made herself a hollow or nest. She settled comfortably under a bush. "If I'd known it was this boring," I said, "I'd have brought my library book."

Mary twiddled grass stalks, sometimes hummed. "My dad says, buck yourself up, Mary, or you'll have to go to reform school."

"What's that?"

"It's where they smack you every day."

"What've you done?"

"Nothing, they just do it."

I shrugged. It sounded only too likely. "Do they smack you on weekends or only school days?"

I felt sleepy. I hardly cared about the answer. "You stand in a queue," Mary said. "When it's your turn . . ." Mary had a little stick which she was digging into the ground, grinding it round and round into the soil. "When it's your turn, Kitty, they have a big club and they beat the holy living daylights out of you. They knock you on the head till your brains squirt out."

Our conversation dried up: lack of interest on my part. In time my legs, folded under me, began to ache and cramp. I shifted irritably, nodded toward the house. "How long do we have to wait?"

Mary hummed. Dug with her stick.

"Put your legs together, Mary," I said. "It's rude to sit like that."

"Listen," she said, "I've been up here when a kid like you is in bed. I've seen what they've got in that house."

I was awake now. "What have they?"

"Something you couldn't put a name to," Mary Joplin said.

"What sort of a thing?"

"Wrapped in a blanket."

"Is it an animal?"

Mary jeered. "An animal, she says. An animal, what's wrapped in a blanket?"

"You could wrap a dog in a blanket. If it were poorly."

I felt the truth of this; I wanted to insist; my face grew hot. "It's not a dog, no, no, no." Mary's voice dawdled, keeping her secret from me. "For it's got arms."

"Then it's human."

"But it's not a human shape."

I felt desperate. "What shape is it?"

Mary thought. "A comma," she said slowly. "A comma, you know, what you see in a book?"

After this she would not be drawn. "You'll just have to wait," she said, "if you want to see it, and if you truly do you'll wait, and if you truly don't you can bugger off and you can miss it, and I can see it all to myself."

After a while I said, "I can't stop here all night waiting for a comma. I've missed my tea."

"They'll be none bothered," Mary said.

SHE WAS RIGHT. I crept back late and nothing was said. It was a summer that, by the end of July, had bleached adults of their purpose. When my mother saw me her eyes glazed over, as if I represented extra effort. You spilled blackcurrant juice on yourself and you kept the sticky patches. Feet grimy and face stained you lived in underbrush and long grass, and each day a sun like a child's painted sun burned in a sky made white with heat. Laundry hung like flags of surrender from washing lines. The light stretched far into the evening, ending in a fall of dew and a bare dusk. When you were called in at last you sat under the electric light and pulled off your sun-

burnt skin in frills and strips. There was a dull roasting
sensation deep inside your limbs, but no sensation as you
peeled yourself like a vegetable. You were sent to bed
when you were sleepy, but as the heat of bedclothes fretted your skin you woke again. You lay awake, wheeling
fingernails over your insect bites. There was something
that bit in the long grass as you crouched, waiting for the
right moment to go over the wall; there was something
else that stung, perhaps as you waited, spying, in the
bushes. Your heart beat with excitement all the short
night. Only at first light was there a chill, the air clear
like water.

And in this clear morning light you sauntered into
the kitchen, you said, casual, "You know there's a house,
it's up past the cemetery, where there's rich people live?
It's got greenhouses."

My aunt was in the kitchen just then. She was pour-
ing cornflakes into a dish and as she looked up some
flakes spilled. She glanced at my mother, and some secret
passed between them, in the flick of an eyelid, a twist at
the corner of the mouth. "She means the Hathaways',"

my mother said. "Don't talk about that." She sounded almost coaxing. "It's bad enough without little girls talking."

"What's bad . . ." I was asking, when my mother flared up like a gas jet: "Is that where you've been? I hope you've not been up there with Mary Joplin. Because if I see you playing with Mary Joplin, I'll skin you alive. I'm telling you now, and my word is my bond."

"I'm not up there with Mary," I lied fluently and fast. "Mary's poorly."

"What with?"

I said the first thing that came into my head. "Ring-worm."

My aunt snorted with laughter.

"Scabies. Nits. Lice. Fleas." There was pleasure in this sweet embroidery.

"None of that would surprise me one bit," my aunt said. "The only thing would surprise me was if Sheila Joplin kept the little trollop at home a single day of her life. I tell you, they live like animals. They've no bedding, do you know?"

"At least animals leave home," my mam said. "The Joplins never go. There just gets more and more of them living in a heap and scrapping like pigs."

"Do pigs fight?" I said. But they ignored me. They were rehearsing a famous incident before I was born. A woman out of pity took Mrs. Joplin a pan of stew and Mrs. Joplin, instead of a civil no-thank-you, spat in it.

My aunt, her face flushed, reenacted the pain of the woman with the stew; the story was fresh as if she had never told it before. My mother chimed in, intoning, on a dying fall, the words that ended the tale: "And so she ruined it for the poor soul who had made it, and for any poor soul who might want to eat it after."

Amen. At this coda, I slid away. Mary, as if turned on by the flick of a switch, stood on the pavement, scanning the sky, waiting for me.

"Have you had your breakfast?" she asked.

"No."

No point asking after Mary's. "I've got money for toffees," I said.

If it weren't for the persistence of this story about

Sheila Joplin and the stew, I would have thought, in later life, that I had dreamed Mary. But they still tell it in the village and laugh about it; it's become unfastened from the original disgust. What a good thing, that time does that for us. Sprinkles us with mercies like fairy dust.

I had turned, before scooting out that morning, framed in the kitchen door. "Mary's got fly-strike," I'd said. "She's got maggots."

My aunt screamed with laughter.

AUGUST CAME AND I remember the grates standing empty, the tar boiling on the road, and fly strips, a glazed yellow studded plump with prey, hanging limp in the window of the corner shop. Each afternoon thunder in the distance, and my mother saying "It'll break tomorrow," as if the summer were a cracked bowl and we were under it. But it never did break. Heat-struck pigeons scuffled down the street. My mother and my aunt claimed, "Tea cools you down," which was obviously not true, but they swigged it by the gallon in their hopeless belief. "It's my only pleasure," my mother said. They sprawled in deck chairs, their white legs stuck out. They held their cigarettes tucked back in their fists like men, and smoke leaked between their fingers. People didn't notice when you came or went. You didn't need food; you got an iced lolly from the shop: the freezer's motor whined.

I don't remember my treks with Mary Joplin, but by five o'clock we always ended, whatever loop we traced, nearby the Hathaways' house. I do remember the feel of my forehead resting against the cool stone of the wall, before we vaulted it. I remember the fine grit in my sandals, how I emptied it out but then there it was again, ground into the soles of my feet. I remember the leather feel of the leaves in the shrubbery where we dug in, how their gauntleted fingers gently explored my face. Mary's conversation droned in my ear: so me dad says, so me mam says . . . It was at dusk, she promised, it was at twilight, that the comma, which she swore was human, would show itself. Whenever I tried to read a book, this summer, the print blurred. My mind shot off across the fields; my mind caressed the shape of Mary, her grinning mouth, her dirty face, her blouse shooting up over her chest and showing her dappled ribs. She seemed to me full of shadows, exposed where she should not be, but then suddenly tugging down her sleeve, shying from a touch, sulking if you jogged her with your elbow: flinching. Her conversation dwelt, dully, on fates that could befall you: beatings, twistings, flayings. I could only think of the thing she was going to show me. And I had prepared my defense in advance, my defense in case I was seen flitting across the fields. I was out punctuating, I would say. I was out punctuating, looking for a comma. Just by myself and not at all with Mary Joplin.

So I must have stayed late enough, buried in the bushes, for I was drowsy and nodding. Mary jolted me with her elbow; I sprang awake, my mouth dry, and I would have cried out except she slapped her paw across my mouth. "Look." The sun was lower, the air mild. In the house, a lamp had been switched on beyond the long windows. One of them opened, and we watched: first one half of the window: a pause; and then the other. Something nudged out into our sight: it was a long chair on wheels, a lady pushing it. It ran easily, lightly, over the stone flags, and it was the lady who drew my attention; what lay on the chair seemed just a dark, shrouded shape, and it was her crisp flowered frock that took my eye, the tight permed shape of her head; we were not near enough to smell her, but I imagined that she wore scent, eau de cologne. The light from the house seemed to dance with her, buoyant, out onto the terrace. Her mouth moved; she was speaking, smiling, to the inert bundle that she pushed. She set the chair down, positioning it carefully, as if on some mark she knew. She glanced about her, turning up her cheek to the mellow, sinking light, then bent to coax over the bundle's head another layer, some coverlet or shawl: in this weather?

"See how she wraps it," Mary mouthed at me.

I saw; saw also the expression on Mary's face, which was greedy and lost, both at once. With a final pat to the blankets, the lady turned, and we heard the click of her heels on the paving as she crossed to the French window, and melted into the lamplight.

"Try and see in. Jump up," I urged Mary. She was

taller than I was. She jumped, once, twice, three times, thudding down each time with a little grunt; we wanted to know what was inside the house. Mary wobbled to rest; she crumpled back to her knees; we would settle for what we could get; we studied the bundle, laid out for our inspection. Its shape, beneath the blankets, seemed to ripple; its head, shawled, was vast, pendant. It is like a comma, she is right: its squiggle of a body, its lolling head.

"Make a noise at it, Mary," I said.

"I dursn't," she said.

So it was I who, from the safety of the bushes, yapped like a dog. I saw the pendant head turn, but I could not see a face; and at the next moment, the shadows on the terrace wavered, and from between the ferns in their great china pots stepped the lady in the flowered dress, and shaded her eyes, and looked straight at us, but did not see. She bent low over the bundle, the long cocoon, and spoke; she glanced up as if assessing the angle of the dying sun; she stepped back, setting her hands on the handles of the chaise, and with a delicate rocking motion she maneuvered it, swayed back and angled it, setting it to rest so that the comma's face was raised to the last warmth; at the same time, bending again and whispering, she drew back the shawl.

And we saw—nothing; we saw something not yet become; we saw something, not a face but perhaps, I thought, when I thought about it later, perhaps a negotiating position for a face, perhaps a loosely imagined notion of a face, like God's when he was trying to form us; we saw a blank, we saw a sphere, it was without feature, it was without meaning, and its flesh seemed to run from the bone. I put my hand over my mouth and cowered, shrinking, to my knees. "Quiet, you." Mary's fist lashed out at me. She caught me painfully. Mechanical tears, jerked out by the blow, sprang into my eyes.

But when I had rubbed them away I rose up, curiosity like a fishhook through my gut, and saw the comma was alone on the terrace. The lady had stepped back into the house. I whispered to Mary, "Can it talk?" I understood, I fully understood now, what my mother had meant when she said at the house of the rich it was bad enough.

To harbor a creature like that! To be kind to the comma, to wrap it in blankets . . . Mary said, "I'm going to throw a stone at it, then we'll see can it talk."

She slid her hand into her pocket, and what she slid out again was a large, smooth pebble, as if fresh from the seashore, the strand. She didn't find that here, so she must have come prepared. I like to think I put a hand on her wrist, that I said, "Mary . . ." But perhaps not. She rose from her hiding place, gave a single whoop, and loosed the pebble. Her aim was good, almost good. We heard the pebble ping from the frame of the chair, and at once a low cry, not like a human voice, like something else.

"I bloody got it," Mary said. For a moment she stood tall and glowing. Then she ducked, she plummeted, rustling, beside me. The evening shapes of the terrace, serene, then fractured and split. With a rapid step the lady came, snapping through the tall arched shadows thrown back by the garden against the house, the shadow of gates and trellises, the rose arbors with their ruined roses. Now the dark flowers on her frock had blown their petals and bled out into the night. She ran the few steps toward the wheeled chair, paused for a split second, her hand fluttering over the comma's head; then she flicked her head back to the house and bawled, her voice harsh, "Fetch a torch!" That harshness shocked me, from a throat I had thought would coo like a dove, like a pigeon; but then she turned again, and the last thing I saw before we ran was how she bent over the comma, and wrapped the shawl, so tender, about the lamenting skull.

IN SEPTEMBER MARY was not at school. I expected to be in her class now, because I had gone up and although she was ten it was known that Mary never went up, just stuck where she was. I didn't ask about her at home, because now that the sun was in for the winter and I was securely sealed in my skin I knew it would hurt to have it pulled off, and my mother, as she had said, was a woman of her word. If your skin is off, I thought, at least they look after you. They lull you in blankets on a terrace and speak softly to you and turn you to the light. I remembered the greed on Mary's face, and I partly understood it, but only partly. If you spent your time trying to understand what happened when you were eight and Mary Joplin was ten, you'd waste your productive years in plaiting barbed wire.

A big girl told me, that autumn, "She went to another school."

"Reform?"

"What?"

"Is it a reform school?"

"Nah, she's gone to daft school." The girl slobbered her tongue out, lolled it slowly from side to side. "You know?"

"Do they slap them every day?"

The big girl grinned. "If they can be bothered. I expect they shaved her head. Her head was crawling."

I put my hand to my own hair, felt the lack of it, the chill, and in my ear a whisper, like the whisper of wool; a shawl around my head, a softness like lamb's wool: a forgetting.

* * *

IT MUST HAVE been twenty-five years. It could have
been thirty. I don't go back much: would you? I saw
her in the street, and she was pushing a buggy, no baby
in it, but a big bag with a spill of dirty clothes coming
out; a baby T-shirt with a whiff of sick, something
creeping like a tracksuit cuff, the corner of a soiled sheet.
At once I thought, well, there's a sight to gladden the
eye, one of that lot off to the launderette! I must tell my
mum, I thought. So she can say, wonders will never
cease.

But I couldn't help myself. I followed close behind
her and I said, "Mary Joplin?"

She pulled the buggy back against her, as if protect-
ing it, before she turned: just her head, her gaze inching
over her shoulder, wary. Her face, in early middle age, had
become indefinite, like wax: waiting for a pinch and a
twist to make its shape. It passed through my mind, you'd
need to have known her well to know her now, you'd need
to have put in the hours with her, watching her sideways. Her skin seemed swagged, loose, and there was
nothing much to read in Mary's eyes. I expected, perhaps,

a pause, a hyphen, a space, a space where a question might follow . . . Is that you, Kitty? She stooped over her buggy, and settled her laundry with a pat, as if to reassure it. Then she turned back to me, and gave me a bare acknowledgement: a single nod, a full stop.

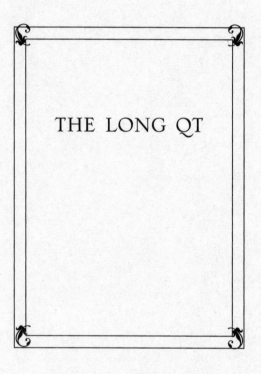

THE LONG QT

He was forty-five when his marriage ended, decisively, on a soft autumn day, the last of the barbecue weather. Nothing about that day was his plan, nothing his intention, though later you could see that every element of the disaster was in place. Above all, Lorraine was in place, standing by the cavernous American fridge, stroking its brushed steel doors with one lacquered fingertip. "Do you ever get in it?" she said. "I mean, on a really hot day?"

"It wouldn't be safe," he said. "Doors could swing shut."

"Jodie would miss you. She'd let you out."

"Jodie wouldn't miss me." He understood it only when he said it. "Anyway," he said. "It's not been that hot."

"No?" she said. "Pity." She stretched up and kissed him on the mouth.

Her wineglass was still in her hand and he felt it roll, cool and damp, against the back of his neck, and make a creeping down his spine. He scooped her against him: a motion of ample gratitude, both hands around her bottom. She murmured something, stretched out an arm to put the glass down, then gave him her whole attention, her open mouth.

He had always known she was available. Only not found her alone, on a warm afternoon, her face a little flushed, three glasses of vinho verde from complete sobriety. Never alone because Lorraine was the sort of girl who moved in a crowd of girls. She was round, kind, down-market for the neighborhood and easy to like. She said droll things, like, "It's so sad to be called after a quiche." She smelled delicious, and of kitchen things: plums and vanilla, chocolate.

He let her go, and as he relaxed his grip he heard her tiny heels click back on the floor. "What a little doll you are," he said. He straightened to his full height. He was able to picture his own expression as he gazed down at her: quizzical, tender, amused; he hardly recognized himself. Her eyes were still closed. She was waiting for him to kiss her again. This time he held her more elegantly, hands on her waist, she on tiptoe, tongue flickering at tongue. Slow and easy, he thought. No rush. But then, crudely, his hand snaked around her back, as if it had a will of its own. He felt for her bra strap. But a twist, a flinch told him, not now, not here. Then where? They could hardly shove through the guests and go upstairs together.

He knew Jodie was rattling about the house. He knew—and he acknowledged this later—that she might at any moment blunder in. She did not like parties that involved open doors, and guests passing between the house and the garden. Strangers might come in, and wasps. It was too easy to stand on the threshold with a burning cigarette, chatting, neither here nor there. You could be burgled where you stood. Picking up glasses, she would push through groups of her own guests, guests who were laughing and passing mobile phones to each other, guests who were, for Christ's sake, trying to relax and enjoy the evening. People would oblige her by knocking back what was in their glass and handing it over. If not she would say, "Excuse me, have you finished with that?" Sometimes they made little stacks of tumblers for her, helpfully, and said, "Here you go, Jodie." They smiled at her indulgently, knowing they were helping her out with her hobby. You would see her off in her own little world, her back to everyone, loading the dishwasher. It was not unknown for her to run a cycle before the party was an hour old. The time would come, after dusk, when wives got maudlin and husbands boastful and bellicose, when spats broke out about private schooling and tree roots and parking permits; then, she said, the less glass there is about, the better. He said, you make it sound like some pub brawl on an estate. He said, for God's sake, woman, put down that wasp spray.

All this he thought, while he was nibbling Lorraine. She nuzzled him and undid his shirt buttons and slid her hand over his warm chest, and let her fingers pause over his heart. If Jodie did come in, he was just going to ask her quietly not to make a scene, to take a deep breath and be more French about it. Then when the people had gone home he would spell it out: it was time she slackened the rein. He was a man at his peak and must see some payoff. He alone by his professional efforts kept them in hand-built kitchens. He was pulling in an amount seriously in excess of anything she could have expected, and his shrewdness had made them near as dammit recession-proof; who could say the same, on their patch? And after all, he was prepared to be fair. "It's not a one-way street," he would say to her. She was a free agent, as he was. She might want an adventure of her own. If she could get one.

He dropped his head to whisper in Lorraine's ear. "When are we going to fuck?"

She said, "How about a week on Tuesday?"

It was then his wife arrived, and paused in the doorway. Her bare arms were drooping stems, and glasses like fruit hung from her finger ends. Lorraine was breathing hotly against his chest, but she must have felt him tense. She tried to pull away, muttering: "Oh bugger, it's Jodie, jump in the fridge." He did not want to part from her; he held her elbows, and for a moment stood and glared at his wife over Lorraine's fluffy head.

Jodie moved a pace or two into the kitchen. But she stopped, her eyes on them, and seemed to freeze. A tiny chime hung in the air, as the glasses shivered in her fingers. She did not speak. Her mouth worked as if she might speak, but only a squeak came out.

Then her hands opened. The floor was limestone and the glass exploded. The crash, the other woman's cry, the splintering light at her feet: these seemed to shock Jodie into reaction. She gave a little grunt, then a gasp, and put her right hand, now empty, onto the slate worktop; then she folded to her knees. "Watch out!" he said. She sunk into the shards as smoothly as if they were satin, as if they were snow, and the limestone gleamed around her, an ice field, each tile with its swollen pillowed edge, each with a shadow pattern faint as breath. She snorted. She seemed dazed, concussed, as if she had smashed a mirror by putting her head through it. She reached out her left hand, and her hand was cut, and a springing well of blood branched into tributaries on her palm. She glanced at it, almost casually, and made a gagging noise. She folded tidily back onto her heels. She fell sideways, her mouth open.

He trod on the glass to get to her, crunching it like ice. He thought this was his chance to slap her, that she was faking to scare him, but when he dragged at her arm it was limp, heavy, and when he shouted Christ Almighty Jodie she didn't flinch, and when he jerked her head round brutally to look into her face, her eyes had already glazed.

So it seemed to him later, when the night's events had to be reprised. He wanted to cry on the shoulder of the ambulance crew and say, only curiosity and mild lust led me on, and a sort of childish defiance, and the fact that it was there for me, on a plate, do you know what I mean? He said, I meant to ask her to be French. Probably she wouldn't have been, but I didn't think she'd fall over like that . . . I mean, how would you? How would you imagine that? And kneeling, kneeling on the glass.

For the first day or so he was not coherent. But nobody was interested in his state of mind; not in the way they would have been, if he had been in custody for killing his wife in some more obvious way. A doctor explained it to him, when they thought he was ready. Long QT syndrome.

A disorder of the heart's electrical activity, which leads to arrhythmia, which leads, in certain circumstances, to cardiac arrest. Genetic, probably. Underdiagnosed, in the population at large. If we spot it early, we doctors can do all sorts of stuff: pacemakers, beta blockers. But there's not much anyone can do, if the first symptom is sudden death. A shock will do it, he said, or strong emotion, strong emotion of any sort. It can be horror. Or disgust. But, then again, it doesn't have to be. Sometimes, he said, people die laughing.

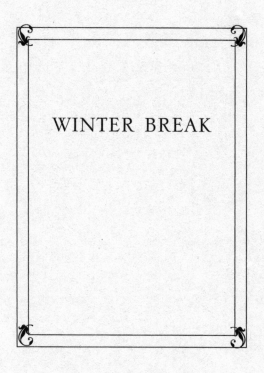

WINTER BREAK

By the time they arrived at their destination, they could no longer recognize their own name. The taxi driver stabbed the air with his placard while they stood gawping up and down the line, until Phil pointed and said, "That's us." Little peaks had grown over the *T*'s in their surname, and the dot on the *i* had drifted away like an island. She rubbed her cheek, numbed by the draught from the air vent above her seat; the rest of her felt creased and gritty, and while Phil bustled toward the man, waving, she picked the cloth of her T-shirt away from the small of her back, and shuffled after him. We dress for the weather we want, as if to bully it, even though we've seen the forecast.

The driver laid a hairy, proprietorial hand on their baggage trolley. He was a squat man with the regulation mustache, and he wore a twill zipped jacket with a tartan lining peeping from under it; as if to say, forget your sunshine illusions. The plane was late and it was already dark. He flung open a rear door for her and humped their bags into the back of his estate car. "Long way," was all he said.

"Yes, but prepaid," Phil said.

The driver plumped down in his seat with a leathery creak. When he slammed his door the whole vehicle shuddered. The front headrests had been wrenched off, so when he swiveled his body to reverse he threw his arm across both seat backs and stared past her unseeing, an inch from her face, while she examined his nostril hair by the giddy flash of the car park's lights. "Sit back, darling," Phil told her. "Seat belt on. Away we go."

How suited he would have been to fatherhood. Whoopsie-daisy. There, there. No harm done.

But Phil thought otherwise. Always had. He preferred to be able to take a winter break during the school term, when hotel rates were lower. For years now he had passed her newspapers, folded to those reports that tell you how children cost a million pounds before they're eighteen. "When you see it set out like that," he'd say, "it's frightening. People think they'll get away with hand-me-downs. Half portions. It doesn't work like that."

"But our child wouldn't have a drug addiction," she'd say. "Not on that scale. It wouldn't be bright enough for Eton. It could go down the road to Hillside Comp. Although, I hear they have head lice."

"And you wouldn't want to deal with that, would you?" he said: a man laying down his ace.

They inched through the town, the pavements jostling, the cheap bars flashing their signs, and Phil said, as she knew he would, "I think we made the right decision." A journey of an hour lay ahead, and they speeded up through the sprawling outskirts; the road began to climb. When she was sure that the driver did not want conversation she eased herself back in her seat. There were two

types of taxi man: the garrulous ones with a niece in
Dagenham, who wanted to talk right the way out to the
far coast and the national park; and the ones who needed
every grunt racked out of them, who wouldn't tell you
where their niece lived if they were under torture. She
made one or two tourist remarks: how had the weather
been? "Raining. Now I smoke," the man said. He thrust
a cigarette right from the packet into his mouth, juggling
a lighter and at one point taking his hands from the
wheel entirely. He drove very fast, treating each swerve in
the road as a personal insult, fuming at any holdup. She
could feel Phil's opinions banking up behind his teeth:
now that won't do the gearbox any good, will it? At first,
a few cars edged past them, creeping down to the lights
of the town. Then the traffic thinned and petered out. As
the road narrowed, black and silent hills fell away behind
them. Phil began to tell her about the flora and fauna
of the high maquis.

She had to imagine the fragrance of herbs crushed
underfoot. The car windows were sealed against the still,
cool night, and she turned her head deliberately away

from her husband and misted the glass with her breath. The fauna was mostly goats. They tumbled down the hillsides, stones cascading after them, and leapt across the path of the car, kids running at their heels. They were patched and parti-colored, fleet and heedless. Sometimes an eye gleamed furtive in a headlight. She twitched at the seat belt, which was sawing into her throat. She closed her eyes.

At Heathrow Phil had been a pain in the security queue. When the young man in front of them bent to pick laboriously at the laces of his hiking boots, Phil said loudly, "He knows he has to take his shoes off. But he couldn't just have slip-ons, like the rest of us."

"Phil," she whispered, "it's because they're heavy. He wants to wear his boots so they don't count as baggage."

"I call it selfish. Here's the queue banking up. He knows what's going to happen."

The hiker glanced up from the tail of his eye. "Sorry, mate."

"One day you'll get your head punched in," she said.

"We'll see, shall we?" Phil said: singing it, like a child in a playground game.

Once, a year or two into their marriage, he had confessed to her that he found the presence of small children unbearably agitating: the unmodulated noise, the strewn plastic toys, the inarticulate demands that you provide something, fix something, though you didn't know what it was.

"On the contrary," she said. "They point. They shout, 'Juice.'"

He nodded miserably. "A lifetime of that," he said. "It would get to you. It would feel like a lifetime."

Anyway, it was becoming academic now. She had reached that stage in her fertile life when genetic strings got knotted and chromosomes went whizzing around and reattaching themselves. "Trisomies," he said. "Syndromes. Metabolic deficiencies. I wouldn't put you through that."

She sighed. Rubbed her bare arms. Phil leaned forward. Cleared his throat, spoke to the driver. "My wife is chilly."

"Wear the cardigan," said the driver. He slotted another cigarette into his mouth. The road now ascended in a series of violent bends, and at each of them he wrenched the wheel, throwing the car's back end out toward the ditches.

"How long?" she asked. "About?"

"Half hour." If he could have concluded the statement by spitting, she felt he would have.

"Still in time for dinner," Phil said encouragingly. He rubbed her arms for her, as if to give encouragement. She laughed shakily. "You make them wobble," she said.

"Nonsense. There's no flesh on you."

There was a cloudy half-moon, a long scoop of fallen land to their right, a bristling treeline above them, and as he cupped her elbow, caressing it, there was once more a skid and slide, a rock shower rattling inconsequentially to the road before them. Phil was just saying, "It'll only take me two minutes to unpack." He was beginning to explain to her his system for traveling light. But the driver grunted, wrenched the wheel, stabbed the brakes and brought them lurching to a halt. She shot forward, jarring her wrist on the seat in front. The seat belt pulled her back. They had felt the impact but seen nothing. The driver swung open his door and ducked out into the night. "Kid," Phil whispered.

Gone under? The driver was pulling something from between the front wheels. He was bent double and they could see his bottom rise in the air, with the frill of tartan at his waist. Inside the body of the car they sat very still, as if not to draw attention to the incident. They did not look at each other, but watched as the driver straightened up, rubbed the small of his back, then walked around and lifted the tailgate, pulling out something dark, a wrapping, a tarpaulin. The chill of the night hit them between their shoulder blades, and fractionally they shrank together. Phil took her hand. She twitched it away; not petulant, but because she felt she needed to concentrate. The driver appeared in silhouette before them, lit by their own headlights. He turned his head and glanced up and down the empty road. He had something in his hand, a rock. He stooped. Thud, thud, thud. She tensed. She wanted to cry out. Thud, thud, thud. The man straightened up. There was a bundle in his arms. Tomorrow's dinner, she thought. Seethed in onion and tomato sauce. She didn't know why the word *seethed* came to her. She remembered a sign down in the town: The Sophocles

School of Motoring. "Call no man happy . . ." The driver posted the bundle into the back of the car, by their luggage. The tailgate slammed.

Recycling, she thought. Phil would say, "Very laudable." If he spoke. But it seemed he had decided not to. She understood that they wouldn't, either of them, mention this dire start to their winter break. She cradled her wrist. Gently, gently. A movement of anxiety. A washing. Massaging the minute pain away. I shall go on hearing it, she thought, at least for the rest of this week: thud, thud, thud. We might make a joke of it, perhaps. How we froze. How we let him get on with it, what else could we . . . because you don't get vets patroling the mountains by night. Something rose into her throat, that she wanted to articulate; tickled her hard palate, fell away again.

THE PORTER SAID, "Welcome to the Royal Athena Sun." Light spilled from a marble interior, and near at hand some cold broken columns were spotlighted, the light shifting from blue to green and back again. That will be the "archaeological feature" as promised, she thought. Another time she would have grinned at the exuberant vulgarity. But the clammy air, the incident . . . she inched out of the car and straightened up, unsmiling, her hand resting on the taxi's roof. The driver nudged past her without a word. He lifted the tailgate. But the porter, hovering helpful, was behind him. He reached for their bags with both hands. The driver moved swiftly, blocking him, and to her own amazement she jumped forward, "No!" and so did Phil, "No!"

"I mean," Phil said. "It's only two bags." As if to prove the lightness of the load, he had gripped one of the bags in his own fist, and he gave it a joyous twirl. "I believe in—" he said. But the phrase *traveling light* eluded him. "Not much stuff," he said.

"Okay, sir." The porter shrugged. Stepped back. She rehearsed it in her mind, as if telling it to a friend, much later: you see, we were made complicit. But the taxi driver didn't do anything wrong, of course. Just something efficient.

And her imaginary friend agreed: still, instinctively

you would feel, you would feel there was something to hide.

"I'm ready for a drink," Phil said. He was yearning for the scene beyond the plate glass: brandy sours, clanking ice cubes in the shape of fish, clicking high heels on terra-cotta tiles, wrought-iron scrollwork, hotel linen, soft pillow. Call no man happy. Call no man happy until he has gone down to his grave in peace. Or at least to his junior suite; and can rub out today and wake tomorrow hungry. The taxi driver leaned into the car to scoop out the second bag. As he did, he nudged aside the tarpaulin, and what she glimpsed—and in the same moment, refused to see—was not a cloven hoof, but the grubby hand of a human child.

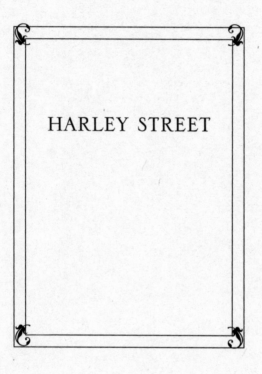

HARLEY STREET

I open the door. It's my job. I have a hundred administrative tasks, and a job title of course, but in effect I'm the meeter and greeter. I take the appointment cards the patients thrust at me—so many of them never say a word—and usher them to the waiting room. Later I send them along the corridor or up the stairs to meet whatever is in store for them: which is usually nothing pleasant.

Mostly they look right through me. Their eyes and ears are closed to everything except their own predicament, and they might just as well be steered in by a robot. I said that one day to Mrs. Bathurst. She turned her eyes on me, in that half-awake manner she has. A robot, she repeated. Or a zombie, I said brightly. That's what our doctors should do, make a zombie. That would cut down on their practice expenses, give them less to complain about.

Bettina, who takes blood in the basement, said what do you mean, make a zombie? Child's play, I said. You need datura, ground puffer fish, then shake up a herbal cocktail to your family recipe. Then you bury them for a bit, dig them up, slap them round the head to stun them: and they're a zombie. They walk and talk, but their will's been taken out.

I was talking on airily, but at the same time, I admit, I was frightening myself. Bettina watched me for signs of madness; her pretty mouth parted, like a split strawberry. And Mrs. Bathurst examined me; her lower jaw sagged, so that the light glinted on one of the gold fillings done cheap for her by Snapper, our dentist.

"What's the matter with you two?" I said. "Don't you read the *New Scientist* these days?"

"My eyes are poor," Mrs. Bathurst said. "I find the TV is company."

Of course, the only thing Bettina buys is *Hello!* She is from Melbourne, and has no sense of humor: no sense of anything really. "Zombies?" she said, articulating carefully: "I thought zombies were for cutting cane under a hot sun. I never associated them with Harley Street."

Mrs. Bathurst shook her head. "Beyond the grave," she said heavily.

Dr. Shinbone (first floor, second left) was passing. "Come, come, nurse," he said, startled. "Is that the sort of talk?"

"She was alluding to the mystery of life and death," I said to Shinbone.

Mrs. Bathurst sighed. "Not such a mystery really."

BETTINA WORKS IN the basement, as I've said, taking samples for the lab. Patients come from practitioners up and down Harley Street, bringing forms with crosses scrawled on them, indicating what tests their blood must have. Bettina extracts some into a tube and puts a label on it. The customers I send her look ill, very ill. They don't like what's coming, but what is it? Just a pinprick. True, we've had some vivisectionists down there, in my time; Bettina is scatty, but skilled in her way, and she doesn't send them out bleeding. Only once, this spring, I remember a young girl stopping by the cubbyhole where I'm housed, and saying oh: staring at a thin trickle of blood, creeping its way from the crook of her elbow toward the swollen blue veins of her wrist. She was seventeen, anorexic, anemic. Her blood should have been as pale as herself, thin and green—but of course it was shockingly fresh and red.

I popped out of my door, and put my hands on her shoulders. I had warm and steady hands, back in May. Down you go, I said to her firmly, run down there to Bettina, and ask her for another plaster. She went. Mrs. Bathurst was crossing the corridor with a kidney bowl in her hand. I saw her gape, and then she put a hand out to the wall, steadying herself. She looked winded, and as pale as the patient. "Dear me!" she said. "Whatever was the matter with that young lass?"

I had to make Mrs. Bathurst a cup of tea. I said, "If blood turns your stomach, why did you go into nursing?"

"Oh no," she said, "no, it doesn't usually take me *that* way at all." She put her hands around her mug and compressed it. "It was just coming upon her there in the hall," she said. "It was so unexpected."

BETTINA IS RED-HAIRED, freckled, creamy. When she sits down her white coat parts, and her short skirts ride up and show her baby-knees. She's adequately pneumatic and brain-dead, and yet she complains of lack of success with men. They often ask her out, but then she has a hard time to understand what's going on. They meet up with other blokes in some noisy pub, and—well, I thought Europe would be different, she says. They talk about motorways. Various junctions, their speed between them, and interesting roadworks they may have met. Toward the end of the evening, a few drinks on board, the men say, we hate Arsenal and we hate Arsenal. The landlord wants people to leave; Bettina leaves too, sliding out by the wall from the Ladies to the nearest exit. "Because not," she says, "I do NOT, want their dribble and their paws on me."

Early in summer, she began to say, men aren't worth it. The television's better; not so repetitive. Or I curl up with a miniseries.

"All the same, you need a hobby," Mrs. Bathurst said. "Something to get you out."

Bettina wears a little silver cross round her neck, on a chain as thin as a thread. "That chain'll snap," Mrs. Bathurst said.

"It's delicate," Bettina said, touching it. In Melbourne, she was drilled to be delicate and sweet. Sometimes she wails, oh jeepers creepers, I think I've mislaid one of my samples, oh, Geronimo H. Jones! Look, calm down, I say, I'm sure you haven't lost any blood at all. Then she counts up her glass tubes, and checks her forms again and everything's okay. One of these days, something will go wrong, she'll mislabel her samples and some great hairy bloke will be told he's estrogen deficient and be invited to attend our Menopause Clinic. Still, if there were complaints, they'd just get lost in the system. The patients shouldn't think that just because they pay for treatment they're due any respect. Sure, it sounds respectful, the way we put it when we send out the bills:

> Dr. Shinbone presents his compliments and
> begs to state that his fee will be:
> 300 guineas

But behind the patients' backs it's more like "Bloody neurotics! Know-alls! Have the nerve to come in here, wanting attention! Asking me questions! Me, a Barts man!"

You probably think I'm cynical, jaundiced. But I've always found Harley Street a hopeless street, very long, very monotonous, the endless railings and the brass plates and the paneled dark doors all the same. I wonder if the patients dream about it as I do, in these sticky summer dawns: as if it stretches not just through space but through time, so that at the end of it there's not Marylebone Road and Cavendish Square, but there's death, and the place you were before you were born. Naturally, I wouldn't mention anything like this to Bettina or Mrs. Bathurst.

For the patients' sake, you have to try to keep cheerful during the day.

Our premises, though, are not designed to lift the spirits. Even if you've never been to Harley Street you've probably got a picture in your mind: leather chesterfields, brass lamps with deep green shades, repro yew coffee tables stacked with *Country Life*—on the whole, an ambience that suggests that if you're terminal you're at least departing in style. Our waiting room is not like that. Our armchairs are assorted types, and greasy where heads and hands have rested. We've even one kitchen chair, with a red plastic seat. As for reading matter—old Shinbone brings in his fishing magazines when he's done with them—*What Maggot?*, that sort of thing. I forget now why we call him Shinbone. Usually we name them by their specialities, and he's not in orthopedics. It must be because of the way his patients look—thinner and thinner, sharpening and sharpening. We see them come in the first time, bluff and flushed, walking bolsters in tweed and cashmere: then we see them get too weak to make it upstairs.

By contrast there's Gland, the top-floor endocrinologist. Gland is a woman who wheezes as she walks. "Make me normal," her patients plead: as if she had any grip on that condition. She treats women for the premenstrual syndrome and for change-of-life upsets: gives them hormones that fatten them up. They come in drawn and wan, hands trembling, very slightly violent and insane— and a couple of months later they're back again, drunkenly cheerful, rolling and puffing, double chinned, ankles bloated, mad eyes sunk into new flesh.

I dwell, as I've said, in a small cave, which has an opening into the hall, a kind of serving hatch. Bettina says, it's like Piccadilly Circus here; she thinks the expression is original. All our time-share doctors come tramping in and out. They put their heads into the hatch and say things like "Miss Todd, the cleaning is unsatisfactory."

I say "Is that so, now?" I reach into my cupboard, and bring out a cloth. "Doctor," I say, "meet the duster. Duster— this is the doctor. You'll be working closely together, from now on."

Cleaning, you'll appreciate, is not my job. It's done in

the night by Mrs. Ranatunga and her son Dennis, when I'm not here to supervise them. Mr. Smear the gynecologist, who is Mrs. Bathurst's employer, is especially obnoxious if his desk doesn't shine. They don't want to pay out, you see, our doctors—but they still want the red-carpet treatment, they expect deference from me like they get from their medical students. Mr. Smear is an ambitious man, Mrs. Bathurst says: works all hours. He lives in Staines—quite near me, but in rather more style—and in the evenings he does abortions at a clinic in Slough. Sometimes when he comes to pick up his post from me I say, "Oh, look, doctor! Your hands are dirty." He'll look huffy, hold them up; but yes, there, there, I say. It's amusing then, to see him wildly stare, and scrutinize his cuffs for blood spots. I take a moral line, you see. I'm not well paid, but I have that luxury.

Our other full-timer is Snapper, whom I mentioned before. He has his own little waiting room, where he puts his patients while their jabs take effect. His trick is to wait until he has one in the chair—a numb-lipped captive, mouth full of fingers—and then start voicing his

opinions. Pakis out, that sort of thing: all the sophistica-
tion you expect from a man with letters after his name. I
send his patients back into the world, their faces lopsided
and their brains fizzing like bombs. Even if they had free
speech, would they contradict him? He might hurt them
next time.

One thing to be said for Snapper—he's not as greedy
as the others. As I said, he gave Mrs. Bathurst a cut-rate
course of treatment.

"Do you have trouble with your teeth, Mrs. Bathurst?"
Bettina asked: her usual tone, all gush and dote.

Mrs. Bathurst said, "When I was a girl they made me
wear a brace. My gums have been tender since." She put
her hand up, as if she were blotting a bead of blood from
her lip. She has long fingers, and horrible stumpy gnawed-
off nails. I thought, it's obvious; she's one of those people
who don't like to talk about their childhood.

I REMEMBER THE day that Mrs. Bathurst appeared at
the door, her CV in her bag: a woman of uncertain age,

sallow, black hair graying, scooped back into wings and pinned with kirby grips. She wore a dark cape—which she carried well, because of her height. She's worn it all summer though: in August, people stare. Perhaps it was part of her uniform once, when she was a hospital nurse. It's the sort of thing that's too good to throw away.

It was late June before she gave me a smile and said, "You can call me Liz." I tried, but I didn't feel easy; for me, I'm afraid, she'll be Mrs. Bathurst forever. Still, I was pleased at the time, that she seemed to want to get on good terms. You see, I've had some problems in my personal life—it's too complicated to go into here—and I suppose I was looking out for an older woman, somebody I could confide in.

One night I said, will you come out? Let's go somewhere! I towed her along to a little French place I used to go to with my boyfriend. It's a gem—old-fashioned, very cheap, and probably the last place in London where the waiters are authentically unpleasant in the Parisian style. I can't say the occasion was relaxed. Mrs. Bathurst didn't seem interested in the food. She spent the eve-

ning perched on the edge of her seat, staring at what the
waiters were carrying through, and sniffing. When the
next table ordered steak tartare, she looked at me: "People
eat that?"

"Apparently."

"What," she said, "anybody?"

"If they can face it."

"Right," she said. She frowned. "I never knew you
could get that."

"You've never lived," I said.

"Oh, yes," she said, "I have."

The bill came, and I said "My treat—really, Liz, hon-
estly." Right, thanks, she said: yanked her cape from the
hook by the door and fluttered off into the night.

I wanted to like her, you see, but she's one of those
people who can't take simple friendship where it's offered.
She was more taken with Bettina—though as far as I
could see then, they had nothing in common. Bettina came
whining to me: "That woman's always hanging about in
my basement."

"Doing what?"

She pouted. "Offering to help me."

"Not a crime."

"Don't you think she's a lesbian?"

"How would I know?"

"I've seen you drinking tea with her."

"Yes, but God blast it. Anyway, Mrs. Isn't she?"

"Oh, Mrs.," Bettina said scornfully. "Probably she's not. She just thinks it sounds more respectful."

"Respectable, you mean."

"Anyway. Lesbians often get married."

"Do they?"

"Definitely."

I said, "I bow to your worldly wisdom."

"Look at her!" Bettina said. "There's something wrong there."

"Thyroid?" I said. "Could be. She's thin. And her hands shake."

Bettina nodded. "Eyes bulge. Mm. Could be."

I feel sorry for both of them. Bettina is on some sort of Grand Tour, earning her way around the old world—she'll stop off and take blood in various European cities, then fly home and settle, she says. Mrs. Bathurst's own relatives live abroad, and she never sees them.

After our meal out—a disaster, probably my fault—I'd have suggested something else—film, whatever—except that, as I've said, I rent a flat in Staines, thirty-five minutes from Waterloo, and Mrs. Bathurst has recently moved from Highgate to Kensal Green. What's it like? I asked her. A hole, she said. Midsummer, she took a fortnight off. She didn't want it, she said, was dreading it in fact—but Smear was going on a sponsored conference, and she wasn't wanted.

The day she was to finish work, she sat with me in my cave, her eyes hidden in her palms. "Mrs. Bathurst," I said, "maybe London's not for you. It's not—I don't find it a kind place myself, it's not a place for women alone." Especially, I didn't say, when they get to your age. After a bit—perhaps she'd been thinking about what I was saying—she took her hands away from her face.

"Move on," she said, "that's the way. Move on, every year or two. That way, you'll always meet somebody, won't you?"

My heart went out to her. I scribbled my address. "Come over, some night. I've got a sofa, I can put you up."

She didn't want to take it, and I pressed it into her hand. What a cold hand she had: cold like an old buried brick. I revised my opinion on the state of her thyroid gland.

SHE DIDN'T COME, of course. I didn't mind—and I mind less, in view of what I know about her now—but I very pointedly didn't ask her what she'd done with her holiday. Her first day back, she looked drained. I said, "What have you been doing, moonlighting?"

She dropped her head, gnawed her lip, turned her big pale face away. She annoyed me, at times; it was as if she didn't understand the English language, the disclaimers and the catchphrases we all have to take on, all of us, wherever we come from. "Anyway," I said, "you've missed all the excitement, Mrs. Bathurst. A week ago we had a break-in." I'd turned up one morning, and there was Mrs. Ranatunga and Dennis. Mrs. Ranatunga was in tears, wringing her J Cloth between her hands. There was a police car outside.

"Could you credit it?" Mrs. Bathurst said. She looked more animated. "Drugs?"

"Yes, that's what Shinbone said. They must have thought we kept stuff on the premises. They ransacked the basement, there was glass all over the place. They practically ripped the fridge door off. They took Bettina's samples, what would they have wanted with them? What would they do with tubes of blood?"

"Can't imagine." Mrs. Bathurst shook her head, as if the human condition was beyond her. "I'll go down and commiserate with Bettina," she whispered. "Poor little girl. What a shock."

ONE SATURDAY, AFTER a long morning at Harley Street, I thought I'd stay in town and go shopping. By two o'clock I was worn out from the heat and the crush. I got on a tour bus, pretended to be a Finnish monoglot, and rested my legs on the empty seat next to me. There was thunder in the air, a clammy heat. Tourists sat dazed on the traffic islands and in the parks. The trees seemed wetly green, foliage hanging in great clumped masses, slow-rustling and heavy. Near Buckingham Palace there was a bed of geraniums—so scarlet, as if the earth had bled through the pavements; I saw the Guardsmen wilting in sympathy, fainting at their posts.

That night it was too hot to sleep. The night following I dreamed that I was in Harley Street. In my dream it was Monday; this is what people usually dream, who work all week. I was coming, or going: the pavement was stained—sunrise or sunset—and I saw that all the Harley Street railings had been filed to points. I had a companion in the street, matching me step for step. I said, look what they've done to the railings. Yes, very nasty points, she said. Then a big hand came out, and pushed me against them.

Next day I was groggy, missed my usual train and arrived at Waterloo twelve minutes late. Twelve minutes—what is it, against the length of a life? It's the start of a foul day, that's what it is—because then comes the scrim-

mage on the Bakerloo line, and Regent's Park station
with the lifts broken down. When I made it to the top I'd
got to sprint—otherwise Smear and Shinbone would have
their heads through my hatch, tapping their watch faces:
Oh, where is Todd? I turned into Harley Street. And what
did I see? Only Liz Bathurst heel-toeing it along. I caught
up, put my hand on her arm: Late, Mrs. Bathurst! This
isn't like you! No sleep, she said, no rest. You too? I said.
My dream was washed away; easily, I melted into sympathy. She nodded. Up all night, she said.

But in the next three, four, five seconds, I began to
feel vastly irritated. I can't put it better than that. God
knows, Bettina wears me down, so amiable and dumb,
and so do the doctors, but in that moment I realized that
Mrs. Bathurst was wearing me down even more. "Liz,"
(and I snapped at her, I admit it) "why do you go around
the way you do? That cape—dump it, can't you? Burn it,
bury it, send it to a car-boot sale. You bloody depress me,
woman. Get your hair done. Buy some emery boards, file
your nails."

My nails, she said, my hair? She turned to me, face

sallow and innocent as the moon. And then without warning—and I realize I must have offended her—drew her arm back, and thumped her fist between my breasts. I careered backward, right into the railings. I felt them dent into my flesh, one bar against my spine and one behind each shoulder blade. Mrs. Bathurst flew off down the street.

I put my hands behind me, wrapping my fingers for a moment around those evil flaking spikes; levered myself away, and staggered after her. If I'd had any faith in our doctors, I might have asked one of them to look at my bruises. But as it was, I just felt shaken up. And sorry, because I'd been brutal—my fatigue was to blame.

All that day I felt raw. The noises of our house seemed amplified. When the doctors scuffed in and out, I could hear their Lobbs scraping the carpets. I could hear Gland's wheezing and puffing; the snarls of her patients, and the sobs of the patients of Smear, as he pushed in with his cold speculum, while Mrs. Bathurst stood by. I heard the whine and grind of Snapper's drill, and the chink of steel instruments against steel dishes.

I said to Bettina, is it Monday all day? Yes, she said; she was so stupid she thought it was a normal question. Ah, I said, then Dr. Lobotomy will be in, 2:30–8:30, first floor second door on the left. I think I'll get a brain operation, or a major tranquilizer or something. I was really nasty to Mrs. Bathurst today. I laughed at her for wearing that cape.

Bettina turned her strawberry mouth down, just at the corners. Her big eyes—unripe fruits—were bulgy with incomprehension. "I know it's old-fashioned," she said, "but I don't see that it's funny."

Should I have noticed at this point, that they'd got together, left me in the cold? I lacked insight this summer—that's how Lobotomy would put it. Yet when the patients come in I seem to see straight through them to the bone. I can hear their hearts flutter, hear their respiration, their digestion, estimate their tick-over speed and say whether they'll be with us for Christmas. It's September now, and I still feel wrecked by London—I am hot, filthy, desperate when I get back to Staines for a bath or shower. For comfort I retain this picture in my mind: one day I'll get further out of town. Somewhere just big enough for me. Somewhere small and quiet.

Next day I bought a bunch of lilies as I came through Waterloo. I pressed them into Mrs. Bathurst's hands. "Sorry," I said. "About the cruel remarks I made." She nodded, absently. She left them on the table in the hall, didn't put them in water; I could hardly do it myself, could I? That evening she and Bettina left together. On her way out she just casually scooped them up, without looking at them. I'll never know if they went home with her or went into a bin.

Next day, Bettina came up from the basement. She stood inside my door, leaning on the frame. She looked faintly bruised and blurred, as if her outline had become fuzzy. "I'd like to talk to you," she said.

"Of course," I said, rather coldly. "Are you in some sort of trouble?"

"Not here," she said, looking around.

"Meet me at one-fifteen," I said. I told her how to find the French place. They're even cheaper at lunchtime.

I was there first. I drank some water. I didn't think she'd come, thought she'd lose the address, lose interest;

her problems were easily soluble, after all. One-thirty, she came flouncing in—cheeks pink with self-importance, coloring when the waiter took her cheap little rain-proof jacket. They brought the menu; she took it without seeing it; she pushed her curly fringe from her forehead and—as I could have forecast—burst into tears. It's been a long, difficult summer. It came to me what Mrs. Bathurst said, about the need to move on: I said, "I suppose you'll not be with us much longer, Bets?"

She locked her eyes onto mine; this surprised me, to see those great blue-violet orbs assume a purpose. "You don't realize, do you?" she said. "My God, when were you born? Don't you realize I'm seeing Bathurst, most nights now?"

Seeing, indeed. I kept a very judicious silence: that's what you should do, if you don't quite know what people mean. Then she did something odd: her elbows on the table, she put her fingers to the back of her neck, and seemed to massage the scalp line there, and raise her roseate hair. It was as if she were trying to show me something. A moment, when her eyes challenged mine, and then her hair fell back against her short white neck. She shivered; she drew one hand across her shoulder, slowly, and allowed it to graze her breast, brush her nipple. One of the old waiters passed and scowled at me, as if he were seeing something he didn't like.

"Oh, come on Bets, don't cry." I extended my hand, let it cover hers for a moment. Okay, so you're that way; I should have known, shouldn't I, when you came into my cave to giggle about sexual perversity? "Lots of people are like it, Bettina."

"Oh, Jesus," she said. All her sweetness had gone; she was foulmouthed, sweating, pallid. "It's like an addiction," she said.

"There are support groups. You can ring up and get advice, about how to come out. I wouldn't have thought it was a problem these days, especially in London. It must be easy enough to find people with the same . . . orientation."

Bettina was shaking her head, her eyes on the check tablecloth. Perhaps it was her family at home she was thinking of; different mores in Melbourne? "Think of it like this—maybe it's just a phase you're going through."

"Phase?" She lifted her head. "That's all you know, Todd. I'm like this forever, now."

Setting aside my prejudices—which is not easy, and why should it be?—I have to say I have no high opinion of Mrs. Bathurst, though as a work colleague she's a lot brighter recently. Now she's hooked up with Bettina, she's energized, brisk. Her eyes are bright and she keeps looking at me. Wants to make amends, I suppose, for attacking me in the street. She's asked me to visit her next weekend. I don't know if I'll go or not. Come for a bite, was how she put it.

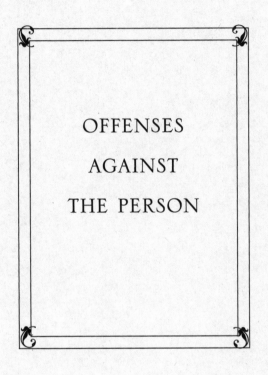

OFFENSES

AGAINST

THE PERSON

Her name was Nicolette Bland, and she was my father's mistress. I'm going back to the early seventies. It's a long time now since he was subject to urges of the flesh. She looked like a Nicolette: dainty, poised, hair short and artfully curling; dark, liquid, slightly slanting eyes. She was honey-colored, as if she'd had a package holiday, and she looked rested, and seldom not-smiling. I put her at twenty-six. I was seventeen, and filling in the summer before university as a junior clerk in my father's chambers. Deviling, he called it. I never knew why.

I used to watch her type, clip-clip: little darting

movements of her pearlescent nails. "They say, Wimmin, never learn to type!" I offered.

They were just beginning to say it, round 1972. "Yes, do they?" she said, a hand hovering for a moment. "Don't start, Vicky. I've a lot to get through by dinnertime." She made a little swatting movement, and got right back to it, *clippety-clip, clop-clip.*

I was fascinated by her feet. I kept hanging my head upside down and peering at them, side by side under the desk. Spike heels had gone out of style, but she stuck by them. Hers were black and very highly polished. Once, when my father came out of his office, she said without looking up—*clip-clop, clickety-clop*—"Frank, do you think we could get a modesty panel affixed to this desk?"

By the time I came back, at Christmas, I got her desk because she had gone to work at Kaplan's, across Albert Square. "Something of a supervisory element to it," my father said. "Also broader scope of work—her experience here, you see, being mostly confined as we are to convey-ancing—"

"Road traffic offenses," I said. "Offenses against the person."

"Yes, that sort of lark. Plus I understand young Simon offered her the extra hundred a year."

"Probably Luncheon Vouchers," I said.

"I shouldn't wonder."

"Occam's Razor shaves you closer," I said. I had only begun to suspect something when he began multiplying explanations. My foot shot out—this happens, when I see the truth suddenly—and hit the modesty panel with a dull thud.

It was all a novelty to me. I knew men had dealings with their secretaries. I imagined there were subspecies of adultery going on, up and down John Dalton Street, Cross Street, Corn Exchange, but we never did matrimonial, or if we did the clerks locked the files away from me, so my most recent take on male duplicity came from the novels of Thomas Hardy. The 1960s were behind us, the era of free love, but it had not dawned in Wilmslow, from where we commuted on weekdays on the crowded 7:45. I guessed why Nicolette had moved across the Square. It was more discreet for a senior partner to keep an affair extramural. The Kaplans must be in on it. Repaying a favor, like the time they sent over a spare stapler when ours came apart in my hand.

Our lives till then had been spotless. We lived in an entirely dust-free house, with a mother occupied full-time in whisking it. My sister had gone to teacher training college. I was of a nature obsessively tidy. As for my father, he was not a man to cause work. Sometimes during that summer he would send me home by myself, saying he must catch up on paperwork—as if there were some other kind of work, like sawing logs, to which a senior partner was bound. He would send with me a message that he would make do with a sandwich when he came in. The brown dinner that my mother was keeping hot for him would shrivel to a stain in its ovenproof serving dish. Solitary in the murk, she would go out into the garden and tie drooping stems to canes, her feet sunk in the earth she had watered earlier. If the telephone rang, "Just coming," she would trill from the gloaming: "See if it's your father." I would hear her knocking the clods off by the back door.

He was on the rota as duty solicitor, and there were nights when he was kept very late at a police station. My mother, who was of a pale nature, would sometimes look paler as the hands of the clock crept round to eleven.

"Shouldn't have to do it," she would snap. "Too senior. Let Peter Metcalfe do it. Let Whatsi Willis do it, he can't be thirty."

When he came in my mother smelled alcohol on his breath. "Surely not risking your license?" She looked brittle.

"It's the atmosphere there at Minshull Street," he said. "It's highly intoxicating."

"You know that girl, Nicolette?" I said. "Is she foreign?"

"Bland," he said: this to my mother. "Nicolette Bland. She used to, whatsit. Typing. Now don't start, Victoria."

"Oh yes," my mother said. "Young Kaplan offered her a pension scheme."

"That's the one. What's this about, all of a sudden? Why would she be foreign?"

"Her nice caramel color. Her little round arms and legs, you know the ones, they look as if they've been molded. As if she was made in Hong Kong."

"I had no idea I was entertaining an Enoch Powellite," he said huffily.

"For crying out loud," I said, "I'd like to know if it's bottled tan, if so where would I get it, I want to be more attractive to the opposite sex and I have to start somewhere."

"You look like a convict with that haircut."

"It wouldn't be my choice," my mother said. "I mean the tan, the haircut goes without saying. Take a look at her palms when next you see her. If it's fake they'll be cocoa-colored in the cracks. Beauty queens have that dilemma. So Valerie says."

Valerie was her hairstylist. She was a formidable perm-ist and neighborhood capo, the Cesare Borgia of the tail comb. My mother had been trying to bring us together. I didn't like the turn the conversation had taken. As if it were me who stood to be questioned. "I'm going to bed."

"I hope you won't have one of your dreams, pet."

"Kissy-kissy," said my father, offering, under the kitchen strip light, his bristling cheek.

AFTER CHRISTMAS, I stayed on in the office while plans were made for my future. Something had gone amiss at university. Though no actual bloodshed. We won't go into it here.

Early in the new year we were in court with an assault that was exciting by our standards. The landlord of a pub in Ancoats was accused of battering one of his customers. The prosecution was ready to say their man had been drinking peaceably at the bar when he felt a call of nature whereupon the landlord willfully misdirected him into the backyard, followed him out and booted him around, unprovoked, among the barrels, finally opening a gate and precipitating him into a drear and filthy ginnel. There stood none other than a uniformed constable, straight and true, who witnessing the gash on his head hastened to take his statement in his ready notebook, in which, by the light of a streetlamp that had just wandered into the ginnel, he wrote an immediate and circumstantial account.

The landlord had brought half his regulars along as witnesses to the mildness of his character. A more cut-throat crew you never saw. There was a great deal that was peculiar about the police account of the night but the landlord, an energetic young Irishman, wasn't helping his case by causing a disturbance in the corridor outside the courtroom, shouting and hallooing and offering to buy a drink for everyone in sight. "Win or lose, sir," he shouted at Bernard Bell, who was prosecuting, "stroll in at any time and name your pleasure."

I had to duck myself, to avoid one of his glad hands. I looked up, steadying myself to follow my papa into court, and to my surprise saw Nicolette appear and then hover at the other end of the corridor. She was frowning, looking about, but when she spotted me she put on a dead-eyed simper. She had some papers in her hand, and she fluttered them, as if suggesting she was on Kaplan business, but somehow I knew she had come to look for my father, I think it was the way her eyes kept roaming, roaming around. "Double gin for you, princess," the land-lord proposed, reeling past her on a policeman's arm. The policeman's face said, now do you see why we opposed bail?

When the landlord, who was a likable sort after all, gave his version of the evening, there was some snigger-ing from the clerks around me, and roars of laughter from the public gallery. Potts, who was sitting and was known for having every element of humor left out of him, threatened to clear the court, so there was soon a hush. But I can't give an account of the case as, just as the police officer took the stand, I felt a kick in my stomach, something like a cloven hoof, and I had to fold myself double to scrabble in the bag at my feet, edge past my father, nod to Potts and back reverently out of the court in the direction of the lavatories. My father, who was now attuned to the biology of young women, gave me a sympathetic glance as I went. I turned at the door, glanced up, and saw that Nicolette was perched in the gallery, squeezed on either side by the landlord's friends, who bounced silently in their seats at every sally in the court below.

When I came back the court had risen for lunch. Nicolette was in the corridor talking earnestly to my father, her face raised to his. The place seemed deserted. My father was somber, eyes fixed on her face. But he must be hungry, I thought. He looked up, he scanned the corridor as if for rescue or a waiter. His eyes passed over me, but he didn't seem to see me. He looked drained, gray, as if he'd been left standing by the curb and one of the lowlifes from Ancoats had been siphoning off his blood.

Then the corridor began to fill up with the bustle of

the various people hurrying back from lunch. A miasma of extinguished cigarettes, of pale ale and cheese and onion and whisky billowed before them, a smell of wet mackintosh and wet newsprint came in with them, as damp pages of the early edition of the *Evening News* were unfolded and flapped in the air. Nicolette clipped over to me, smiling, her heels spearing the floor. She seemed keen to strike up a friendship. She clicked open her bag. "Your father thought you might need two of these." She pulled out a bottle of aspirin.

"I usually have three."

"Be my guest."

She unscrewed the top with an air of liberality. But there was a cotton wool twist in the neck of the bottle, and when I tried to fish it out it flinched away from my forefinger and impacted itself out of reach. "Give it here," Nicolette said. She probed the glass with her pearly claw. "The little bugger," she said.

My father had joined us. Holding up his thick digit, he showed that he was helpless in the matter. Nicolette flushed, her face downturned. Across each eyelid there ran an eely flick, teal-blue, drawn with a fine pen. I positioned myself next to her so that I could try to see down her neckline, and find out where her caramel hue ended, but all I could see was an ugly mottling of frustration, spreading crimson to where the buttons of her silk blouse blocked my view.

The forces of the Crown arrived. "What's up, Frank?" Bernard Bell said.

My father said, "My daughter's started her . . . she's started her headache."

"Touch of the sun." It was February. Nobody smiled. "Oh, suit yourselves," Bernard said. "Tweezers will do it."

I almost glanced behind me for Tweezers, a rachitic clerk with fingerless gloves. Then I saw that Bernard was digging in his pockets. He came out with some treasury tags, small predecimal currency and some fluff. He sifted it, plunged his two hands in again, and ferreted down there for quite a while; it was a tribute, I thought, to the charms of Nicolette. My father snorted, "Bernie, you never carry tweezers into court? Nail-clippers, yes . . ."

"You may scoff," Bernie said, "but I have known nasty

injuries occur from slivers of flying glass, where in the hands of a man trained by the St. John Ambulance, a handy pair of sterilized . . ."

But then Nicolette gave a squeak of triumph. She held up the plug of cotton wool between her fingertips. Three aspirin rolled into my palm. If they'd rolled into her palm, I could have settled a question.

Early in the afternoon the case was thrown out. The Irishman tumbled into the corridor to greet his well-wishers, punching the air and crying, "Drinks all round."

It surprised me to see that Nicolette was still there. She was standing alone, her bag looped over her elbow. She'd lost her papers, whatever they were. She looked as if she were queuing up for something. "Very honorably prosecuted, sir, and in a gentlemanlike manner," the landlord flung in the Crown's direction. When he passed Nicolette, fists flailing, feet flashing out, I saw her step back against the wall with a briskness almost military, and clamp her forearm across her tiny belly.

That night my father took my mother aside. She kept walking away from him, in little aimless drifts, so he had to follow her down the hall and into the kitchen, saying listen to me Lillian. I went up to the bathroom and looked in the bathroom cabinet, which I normally avoided as the thought made me sick. I sorted through what was in there: a small bottle of olive oil, some oozing ointments, a roll of sticking plaster and some round-ended scissors with a rust spot at the junction of their blades: crepe bandages packed in cellophane. There was more provision for casualties than I had imagined. I pulled some cotton wool out of a packet, rolled it up into balls, and put it in my ears. I went downstairs. I watched my soundless feet go before me, like scouts. I didn't look through the kitchen door, though it had a glass panel. But after a while I sensed a vibration under my feet, as if the whole house were shaking.

I went into the kitchen. My father wasn't there and being quick on the uptake I deduced he must have slipped out through the back door. The room was filled with a dull thudding sound. My mother was beating on the edge of the kitchen table the ovenproof dish in which she usually shriveled his dinner. It was made of toughened glass and took a long time to break. When it shattered at last she left the wreckage on the floor and brushed past me on her way upstairs. I pointed to my ears, as if to warn her that any commentary on the situation was wasted on me. But left to myself I picked up all the shards of the dish, and carried on picking them up and placing them on the table. Not having the obliging tweezers by me I took up the fragments from the carpet tiles with my fingernails. This detailed work of recovery occupied a satisfactory amount of time. While the muffled evening continued on its way without me I arranged the jagged fragments so that the pattern of onions and carrots with which the dish had been decorated was complete again. I left it for her to find, but when I came down next morning it was gone as if it had never been.

I WENT ROUND to see them after the twins were born. Nicolette was very pally. She tried to reminisce about old times—the modesty panel, all that—but I firmly rebuffed her. My father still looked gray, as he had since the day the Irish landlord was in court, and the babies were both yellow, but he seemed pleased with them, grinning away like a callow youth, I thought. I looked at their little fingers, and the palms of their hands, and marveled at them, as you are meant to do, and he seemed all right with that. "How's your mother?" he said.

Something was stewing, a brown foodstuff, on the hot plate of the Baby Belling.

My mother got the house. She said she would have been loath to leave the garden. He had to pay her maintenance, and she spent some of it on yoga classes. Having been a brittle person, she became flexible. Each day she saluted the sun.

I was not a prejudiced young person. I still notice these things, the colors people turn when they're lying, the colors they turn. Nicolette, I saw, looked as if she needed dusting. She smelled of baby sick and brown stewing, and her curly hair hung above her ears in woolly clumps. She whispered to me, "Sometimes he's on call, you know, the rota. He's out till all hours. Did he do that before?"

My father, always a diffident man, was agitating his knees beneath his babes, by way of bouncing them. He was singing to them, in a subfusc way: "One-a-penny two-a-penny, hot cross buns." Love is not free. In point of fact, he was reduced to penury, but he must have counted on that. I expect Simon Kaplan admired him, Bernard Bell, those people. As far as I could see, everybody but me had got what they had ordered. "Drinks all round?" I said. Nicolette, finding her hands free, reached into the sideboard and extracted a bottle of British sherry. I watched her blow the dust off it. Only I had failed to name my pleasure.

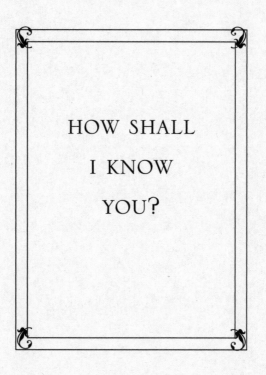

HOW SHALL

I KNOW

YOU?

One summer at the fag end of the nineties, I had to go out of London to talk to a literary society, of the sort that must have been old-fashioned when the previous century closed. When the day came, I wondered why I'd agreed to it; but yes is easier than no, and of course when you make a promise you think the time will never arrive: that there will be a nuclear holocaust, or something else diverting. Besides, I had a sentimental yearning for the days of self-improvement; they were founded, these reading clubs, by master drapers and their shopgirl wives; by poetasting engineers, and uxorious physicians with long winter evenings to pass. Who keeps them going these days?

I was leading at the time an itinerant life, struggling with the biography of a subject I'd come to dislike. For two or three years I'd been trapped into a thankless cycle of picking up after myself, gathering in what I'd already gathered, feeding it onto computer disks that periodically erased themselves in the night. And I was forever on the move with my card indexes and my paper clips, and my cheap notebooks with their porous, blotchy pages. It was easy to lose these books, and I left them in black cabs or in the overhead racks of trains, or swept them away with bundles of unread newspapers from the weekends. Sometimes it seemed I'd be forever compelled to retrace my own steps, between Euston Road and the newspaper collections, which in those days were still in Colindale; between the rain-soaked Dublin suburb where my subject had first seen the light and the northern manufacturing town where—ten years after he ceased to be use or ornament—he cut his throat in a bathroom of a railway hotel. "Accident," the coroner said, but there's a strong suspicion of a cover-up; for a man with a full beard, he must have been shaving very energetically.

* * *

I WAS LOST and drifting that year, I don't deny it. And as my bag was always packed, there was no reason to turn down the literary society. They would ask me, they said, to give their members a snappy summary of my researches, to refer briefly to my three short early novels, and then answer questions from the floor: after which, they said, there would be a Vote of Thanks. (I found the capitals unsettling.) They would offer a modest fee—they said it—and lodge me for bed and breakfast at Rosemount, which was quietly situated, and of which, they said enticingly, I would find a photograph enclosed.

This photograph came in the secretary's first letter, double-spaced on small blue paper, produced by a typewriter with a jumping *h*. I took Rosemount to the light and looked at it. There was a suspicion of a Tudor gable, a bay window, a Virginia creeper—but the overall impression was of blurring, a running of pigment and a greasiness at the edges, as if Rosemount might be one of those ghost houses that sometimes appear at a bend in the road, only to melt away as the traveler limps up the path.

So I was not surprised when another blue letter came, hiccupping in the same way, to say that Rosemount was closing for refurbishments and they would be obliged to use Eccles House, convenient for the venue and they understood quite reputable. Again, they enclosed a photograph: Eccles House was part of a long white terrace, four stories high, with two surprised attic windows. I was touched that they felt they ought to illustrate the accommodation in this way. I never cared where I stayed as long as it was clean and warm. I had often, of course, stayed in places that were neither. The winter before there had been a guesthouse in a suburb of Leicester, with a smell so repellent that when I woke at dawn I was unable to stay in my room for longer than it took me to dress, and I found myself, long before anyone else was awake, setting my booted feet on the slick wet pavements, tramping mile after mile down rows of semidetached houses of blackening pebbledash, where the dustbins had wheels but the cars were stacked on bricks; where I turned at the end of each street, and crossed, and retrod my tracks, while behind thin curtains East Midlanders turned and muttered in their sleep, a hundred and a hundred then a hundred couples more.

In Madrid, by contrast, my publishers had put me in a hotel suite that consisted of four small dark paneled rooms. They had sent me an opulent, unwieldy, scented bouquet, great wheels of flowers with woody stems. The concierge brought me heavy vases of a grayish glass, slippery in my hands, and I edged them freighted with blooms onto every polished surface; I stumbled from room to room, coffinned against the brown paneling, forlorn, strange, under a pall of pollen, like a person trying to break out from her own funeral. And in Berlin, the desk clerk had handed me a key with the words "I hope your nerves are strong."

THE WEEK BEFORE the engagement, my health was not good. There was a continuous airy shimmer in my field of vision, just to the left of my head, as if an angel were trying to appear. My appetite failed, and my dreams took me to strange waterfronts and ships' bridges, on queasy currents and strange washes of the tide. As a biographer I was more than usually inefficient; in untangling my subject's accursed genealogy I mixed up Aunt Virginie with the one who married the Mexican, and spent a whole hour with a churning stomach, thinking that all my dates were wrong and believing that my whole Chapter Two would have to be reworked. The day before I was due to travel east I simply gave up on the whole enterprise, and lay on my bed with my eyes shut tight. I felt not so much a melancholy, as a kind of general insufficiency. I seemed to be pining for those three short early novels, and their brittle personnel. I felt a wish to be fictionalized.

My journey was uneventful. Mr. Simister, the secretary, met me at the station. How shall I know you? he had said on the telephone. Do you look like the photograph on your book jackets? Authors, I find, seldom do. He giggled after saying this, as if it were edgy wit of a high order. I had considered: a short pause on the line had made him ask, Still there? I am the same, I said. They are not a bad likeness, only I am older now, of course, thinner in the face, my hair is much shorter and a different color, and I seldom smile in quite that way. I see, he said.

"Mr. Simister," I asked, "how shall I know you?"

I KNEW HIM by his harassed frown, and the copy of my first novel, *A Spoiler at Noonday*, which he held across his heart. He was buttoned into an overcoat; we were in June, and it had turned wintry. I had expected him to hiccup, like his typewriter.

"I think we shall have a wet one of it," he said, as he led me to his car. It took me a little time to work my way through this syntactical oddity. Meanwhile he creaked and ratcheted car seats, tossed a soiled evening newspaper onto the dog blanket in the back, and vaguely flapped his hand over the passenger seat as if to remove lint and dog hairs by a magic pass. "Don't your members go out in the rain?" I said, grasping his meaning at last.

"Never know, never know," he replied, slamming the door and shutting me in. My head turned back,

automatically, the way I had come. As, these days, my
head tends to do.

We drove for a mile or so, toward the city center. It
was five-thirty, rush hour. My impression was of an arte-
rial road, lined by sick saplings, and lorries and tankers
rumbling toward the docks. There was a huge, green
roundabout, of which Mr. Simister took the fifth exit, and
reassured me, "Not far now."

"Oh, good," I said. I had to say something.

"Are you not a good traveler?" Mr. Simister said anx-
iously.

"I've been ill," I said. "This last week."

"I'm sorry to hear that."

He did look sorry; perhaps he thought I would be
sick on his dog blanket.

I turned away deliberately and watched the city. On
this wide, straight, busy stretch, there were no real shops,
just the steel-shuttered windows of small businesses. On
their upper floors at smeary windows were pasted Day-
Glo banners that said TAXI TAXI TAXI. It struck me as an
area of free enterprise: freelance debt collectors, massage

parlors, body shops and money launderers, dealers in seedy accommodation let twice and thrice, bucket shops for flights to Miami or Bangkok, and netted yards where inbred terriers snarl and cars are given a swift respray before finding a happy new owner. "Here we are." Mr. Simister pulled up. "Like me to come in?"

"No need," I said. I looked around me. I was miles from anywhere, traffic snarling by. It was raining now, just as Mr. Simister had said it would. "Half past six?" I asked.

"Six-thirty," he said. "Nice time for a wash and brushup. Oh, by the way, we're renamed now, Book Group. What do you think? Falling rolls, you see, members dead."

"Dead? Are they?"

"Oh yes. Get in the younger end. You're sure you wouldn't like a hand with that bag?"

ECCLES HOUSE WAS not precisely as the photograph had suggested. Set back from the road, it seemed to grow out of a parking lot, a jumble of vehicles double-parked and crowding to the edge of the pavement. It had once been a residence of some dignity, but what I had taken to be stucco was in fact some patent substance newly glued to the front wall: it was grayish-white and crinkled, like a split-open brain, or nougat chewed by a giant.

I stood on the steps and watched Mr. Simister edge into the traffic. The rain fell harder. On the opposite side of the road there was a carpet hangar, with the legend ROOM-SIZED REMNANTS painted on a banner on its façade. A depressed-looking boy zipped into his waterproofs was padlocking it for the night. I looked up and down the road. I wondered what provision they had made for me to eat. Normally, on evenings like this, I would make some excuse—a phone call expected, a nervous stomach—and turn down the offer of "a bit of dinner." I never want to prolong the time I spend with my hosts. I am not, in fact, a nervous woman, and the business of speaking to a hundred people or so causes me no qualms, but it is the small talk afterward that wears me down, and the twinkling jocular-ity, the "book-chat" that grates like a creaking hinge.

So I would sneak away; and if I had not been able to persuade the hotel to leave me some sort of supper tray, I would walk out and find a small, dark, half-empty restaurant, at the end of a high street, that would provide a dish of pasta or a fillet of sole, a half-bottle of bad wine, a diesel-oil espresso, a glass of Strega. But tonight? I would have to go along with whatever arrangement they had made for me. Because I could not eat carpets, or "personal services," or solicit a bone from a drug dealer's dog.

MY HAIR FLATTENED by the rain, I stepped inside, to a travelers' stench. I was reminded at once of my visit to Leicester; but this place, Eccles House, was on a stifling scale of its own. I stood and breathed in—because one must breathe—tar of ten thousand cigarettes, fat of ten thousand breakfasts, the leaking metal seep of a thousand shaving cuts, and the horse-chestnut whiff of nocturnal emissions. Each odor, ineradicable for a decade, had burrowed into the limp chintz of the curtains and into the scarlet carpet that ran up the narrow stairs.

At once I felt my guardian angel flash, at the corner of my eye. The weakness he brought with him, the migrainous qualm, ran through my whole body. I put out the palm of my hand and rested it against the papered wall.

There seemed to be no reception desk, nowhere to sign in. Probably no point: who'd stay here, who traveled under their right name? Come to that, I didn't travel under mine. Sometimes I got confused, what with the divorce disentanglements, and the business bank accounts, and the name under which I'd written my early novels, which happened to be the name of one of my grandmothers. You should be sure, when you start in this business, that there's one name you can keep: one that you feel entitled to, come what may.

From somewhere—beyond a door, and another door— there was a burst of male laughter. The door swung shut; the laughter ended in a wheeze, which trailed like another odor on the air. Then a hand reached for my bag. I looked down, and saw a small girl—a girl, I mean, in her late teens: a person, diminutive and crooked, banging my bag against her thigh.

She looked up and smiled. She had a face of feral sweetness, its color yellow; her eyes were long and dark, her mouth a taut bow, her nostrils upturned as if she were scenting the wind. Her neck seemed subject to a torsion; the muscles on the right side were contracted, as if some vast punitive hand had picked her up and taken her in a grip. Her body was tiny and twisted, one hip thrust out, one leg lame, one foot trailing. I saw this as she broke away from me, lugging my bag toward the stairs.

"Let me do that." I carry, you see, not just the notes of whatever chapter I am working on, but also my diary, and those past diaries, kept in A4 spiral notebooks, that I don't want my current partner to read while I'm away: I think carefully about what would happen if I were to die on a journey, leaving behind me a desk stacked with ragged prose and unpunctuated research notes. My bag is therefore small but leaden, and I rushed to catch up with her, wanting to drag it from her poor hand, only to realize that the scarlet stinking stairs shot steeply upward, their risers deep enough to trip the unwary, and took a sharp twist that brought us to the first landing. "Up to the top," she said. She turned to smile over her shoulder. Her face swiveled to a hideous angle, almost to where the back of her head had been. With a fast, crabwise scuttle, leaning on the side of her built-up shoe, she shot away toward the second floor.

She had lost me, left me behind. By that second landing, I was not in the race. As I began to climb to the third floor—the stairs now were like a ladder, and the smell was more enclosed, and had clotted in my lungs—I felt again the flash of the angel. I was short of breath, and this made me stop. "Only a few more," she called down. I stumbled up after her.

On a dark landing, she opened one door. The room was a sliver: not even a garret, but a bit of corridor blocked off. There was a sash window that rattled, and a spiritless divan with a brown cover, and a small brown chair with a plush buttoned back, which—I saw at once—had a gray rime of dust, like navel fluff, accumulated behind each of its buttons. I felt sick, from this thought, and the climb. She turned to me, her head wobbling, her expression dubious. In the corner was a plastic tray, with a small electric kettle of yellowed plastic; yellowed wheat ears decorated it. There was a cup.

"All this is free," she said. "It is complimentary. It is included."

I smiled. At the same time, inclined my head, modestly, as if someone were threading an honor around my neck.

"It is in the price. You can make tea. Look." She held up a sachet of powder. "Or coffee."

My bag was still in her hand; and looking down, I saw that her hands were large and knuckly, and covered, like a man's, with small unregarded cuts.

"She doesn't like it," she whispered. Her head fell forward onto her chest.

It was not resignation; it was a signal of intent. She was out of the room, she was hurtling toward the stair head, she was swarming down before I could draw breath.

My voice trailed after her. "Oh, please . . . really, don't . . ."

She plunged ahead, and around the bend in the stairs. I followed, I reached out, but she lurched away from me. I took a big ragged breath. I didn't want to go down, you see, if I might have to come up again. In those days I didn't know there was something wrong with my heart. I only found it out this year.

WE WERE BACK on the ground floor. The child produced from a pocket a big bunch of keys. Again, that bilious laughter washed out, from some unseen source. The door she opened was too near this laughter, far too near for my equanimity. The room itself was identical, except that a kitchen smell was in it, deceptively sweet, as if there were a corpse in the wardrobe. She put down my bag on the threshold.

I felt I had come a long way that day, since I had crept out of my double bed, the other side occupied by a light sleeper who still seemed, sometimes, a stranger to me. I had crossed London, I had traveled east, I had been up the stairs and down. I felt myself too proximate, now, to the gusty, beery laughter of unknown men. "I'd rather . . ." I said. I wanted to ask her to try for an intermediate floor. Perhaps not all the rooms were empty, though? It was the other occupants I didn't like, the thought of them, and I realized that here on the ground floor I was close to the bar, to the slamming outer door letting in the rain and the twilight, to the snarled-up traffic . . . She picked up my bag. "No . . ." I said. "Please. Please don't. Let me . . ."

But she was off again, swaying at speed toward the stairs, dragging her leg after her, like an old rebuff. I heard her draw breath above me. She said, as if just to herself, "She thought it was worse."

I caught up with her inside the first choice of room. She leaned against the door. She showed no sign of discomfort, except that one eyelid jerked in spasm; the corner of her lip lifted in time with it, pulling away from her teeth. "I'll be all right here," I said. My ribs were heaving with effort. "Let's not do any more rooms."

I felt a sudden wash of nausea. The migraine angel leaned hard on my shoulder and belched into my face. I wanted to sit down on the bed. But courtesy demanded something. The child had put down my bag, and without it she looked even more unbalanced, her vast hands hanging, her foot scuffling the floor. What should I do? Ask her to stay for a cup of tea? I wanted to offer her money but I couldn't think what would be enough for such a feat of porterage, and besides I thought that I might be further in debt to her before I left the place, and perhaps it was best to run up a tab.

I FELT SAD, as I stood in the doorway, waiting for Mr. Simister. My nose ran a little. When Mr. Simister arrived I said, "I have hay fever."

"We are actually close," he said; then, after a long pause: "To the venue." We could walk, he was saying. I shrank back into the doorway. "Perhaps in view of your ailments," he said. I shrank inside: how did he know my ailments? "Though, a night like this," he said. "Damps the pollen down. I'd have thought. Somewhat."

The lecture was to be given at what I can only describe as a disused school. There were school corridors, and those polished shields on the wall that say things like "JK Rowling, Cantab 1963." There was a smell of school, residual—polish and feet. But there were no signs of actual, present-day pupils. Perhaps they had all fled into the hills, and left it to the Book Group.

Despite the rain, the members had come out in heroic numbers: twenty, at least. They were widely dispersed through the long rows, with tactful gaps between: in case the dead ones rolled in late. Some few had squints and others sticks, many had beards including the women, and the younger members—even those who appeared sound at first glance—had a glazed unfocused eye, and bulging parcels under their seats, which I knew at once would be the manuscripts of sci-fantasy novels, which they would like me to take away and read and comment on and post back to them—"In your own time, of course."

There is a way of looking, and then there is a professional, impersonal, way of looking. I settled myself behind a table, took a sip of water, flicked through my notes, checked the location of my handkerchief, raised my head, scanned the room, attempted a theoretical sort of eye contact, and swept a smile from side to side of the audience: looking, I am sure, like one of those nodding dogs you used to see in the back of Austin Maestros. Mr. Simister got to his feet; to say "he stood up" would give you no notion of the impressive performance it really was. "Our guest has not been well in the last week, you will be as sorry as I am to learn, hay fever, so will deliver her lecture sitting down."

I felt a fool already, a greater fool than I needed to feel. Nobody would sit down because they had hay fever. But I thought, never explain. I rattled smartly through my performance, throwing in the odd joke and working in one or two entirely spurious local allusions. Afterward there were the usual questions. Where did the title of your first book come from? What happened to Joy at the end of *Teatime in Bedlam*? What, would I say, looking back, were my own formative influences? (I replied with my usual list of obscure, indeed nonexistent Russians.) A man in the front row spoke up: "May I ask what prompted your foray into biography, Miss Er? Or should I say Ms.?" I smiled weakly, as I always do, and proffered "Why don't you call me Rose?" Which created a little stir, as it is not my name.

On the way back Mr. Simister said that he considered it a great success, more than somewhat, and was sure they were all most grateful. My hands were clammy from the touch of the science fantasists, there was a felt-tip mark on my cuff, and I was hungry.

'By the way, I expect you have eaten,' Mr. Simister said. I sank down in my seat. I didn't know why he should expect anything of the sort, but I made an instant decision in favor of starvation, rather than go to some establishment with him where the members of the Book Group might be lurking under a tablecloth or hanging from a hat stand, upside down like bats.

I stood in the hall of Eccles House, and shook drops of water from myself. There was an immanent odor of aged cooking oil. Supper over, then: all chips fried? An indoor smog hovered, about head height. From the shadows at the foot of the stairs, the small girl materialized. She gazed up at me. "We don't normally get ladies," she said. Her tongue, I realized, was too big for her mouth. She had a rustle in her speech, as if the god that made her was rubbing his dry palms together.

"What are you doing?" I said. "Why are you, why are you still on duty?"

There was a clatter behind a half-open door, the bump and rattle of bottles knocked together, and then the scraping of a crate across the floor. A second later, "Mr. Webley!" someone called.

Another voice called, "What the fuck now?" A small dirty man in a waistcoat tumbled out of an office, leaving the door gaping on a capsizing tower of box files. "Ah, the writer!" he said.

It wasn't I who had called him out. But I was enough to make him linger. Perhaps he thought he was going to filch the regular writer business from Rosemount. He stared at me; he walked around me for a while; he did everything but finger my sleeve. He rose on his toes and thrust his face into mine.

"Comfortable?" he asked.

I took a step backward. I trampled the small girl. I felt the impress of my heel in flesh. She wormed her flinching foot from under mine. She uttered not a sound.

"Louise—" the man said. He sucked his teeth, considering her. "Fuck off out of it," he said.

* * *

I BOLTED UPSTAIRS then, stopping only on the second landing. The whole evening was taking on a heightened, crawling quality. These men called sinister and webley; I thought they might know each other. I have to face a night in that room, I thought, with no company, and see what sort of sheets they keep beneath that turd-colored candlewick cover. For a moment I was uncertain whether to go up or down. I'd not sleep if I didn't eat, but out there was the rain, a moonless night in a strange town, miles from the center and I have no map; I could send for a taxi and tell the driver to take me somewhere to eat, because that's what they do in books, but people never do in life, do they?

I stood debating this with myself, and saying come now, come now, what would Anita Brookner do? Then I saw something move, above me; just a faint stir of the air, against the prevailing fug. My left eye was by now malfunctioning quite badly, and there were jagged holes in the world to that side of my head, so I had to turn my whole body to be sure of what I saw. There in the darkness was the small girl, standing above me. How? My poor heart—not yet diagnosed—gave one sunken knock against my ribs; but my head said coolly, emergency stairs? Goods lift?

She came down, silent, intent, the worn tread muffling the scrape of her shoe. "Louise," I said. She put her hand on my arm. Her face, turned up toward me, seemed luminous. "He always says that," she murmured. "Eff off out."

"Are you related to him?" I asked.

"Oh no." She wiped some drool from her chin. "Nothing like that."

"Don't you get time off?"

"No, I have to clear the ashtrays last thing, I have to wash up in the bar. They laugh at me, them men. Saying, han't you got a boyfriend, Louise? Calling me, 'Hippy.'"

IN THE ROOM, I hung my coat on the outside of the wardrobe, ready to go; it is a way of cheering myself up, that I learned in the hotel in Berlin. My cheeks burned. I could feel the sting of the insults, the sniggering day by day; but "Hippy" seemed a mild name, when you consider . . . The appalling thought came to me that she was some sort of test. I was like a reporter who finds an orphan in a war zone, some ringwormed toddler squawking in the ruins. Are you supposed to just report on it; or pick up the creature and smuggle it home, to learn English and grow up in the Home Counties?

THE NIGHT, PREDICTABLY, was shot through with car alarms, snatches of radio playing from other rooms, and the distant roaring of chained animals. I dreamed of Rosemount, its walls fading around me, its bay windows melting into air. Once, half-awake, tossing under the fungoid counterpane, I thought I smelled gas. I tumbled into sleep again and smelled gas in my dream: and here were the members of the Book Group rolling from beneath my bed, sniggering as they plugged the chinks round the windows and door with the torn pages of their manuscripts. Gasping, I woke. A question hovered in the fetid air. Just what *did* prompt your foray into biography, Miss Er? Come to that, what prompted your foray into foraying? What prompted anything at all?

I was downstairs by six-thirty. The day was fine. I

was hollow at my center, and in a vicious temper. The door stood open, and a wash of light ran over the carpet like sun-warmed margarine.

My taxi—prebooked, as always, for a quick getaway—was at the curb. I looked around, cautious, for Mr. Webley. Already a haze was beginning to overlay Eccles House. Smokers' coughs rattled down the passages, and the sound of hawking, and the flushing of lavatories.

Something touched my elbow. Louise had arrived beside me, noiseless. She wrested the bag from my hand. "You came down by yourself," she whispered. Her face was amazed. "You should have called me. I'd have come. Are you not having your breakfast?"

She sounded shocked, that anyone should refuse food. Did Webley feed her, or did she scavenge? She raised her eyes to my face, then cast them down. "If I hadn't just come now," she said, "you'd have gone. And never said bye-bye."

We stood at the curb together. The air was mild. The driver was reading his *Star*. He didn't look up.

"Might you come back?" Louise whispered.

"I don't think so."

"I mean, one of these days?"

I never doubted this: if I told her to get into the taxi, she would do it. Away we'd go: me rattled, afraid of the future; her trusting and yellow, her mad eyes shining into mine. But what then? I asked myself. What would we do then? And have I the right? She is an adult, however short. She has a family somewhere. I stared down at her. Her face, in full daylight, was patchily jaundiced as if dyed with cold tea; her broad smooth forehead was mottled with deeper blotches, the size and color of old copper coins. I could have wept. Instead, I took my purse out of my bag, peered inside it, took out a twenty-pound note, and squeezed it into her hand. "Louise, will you buy yourself something nice?"

I didn't look into her face. I just got into the taxi. My migraine aura was now so severe that the world on the left had ceased to exist, except as an intermittent yellow flash. I was nauseated, by inanition and my own moral vacuity. But by the time the cab crawled up to the station approach, I was getting a bit satirical, *faute de mieux*, and thinking, well, for sure A. S. Byatt would have managed it better: only I can't quite think how.

When I got to the station, and paid the driver, I found I had only £1.50 left. The cash machine was out of order. Of course, I had a credit card, and if there had been a dining service I could have paid for my breakfast on board. But there was, the announcement said, "a buffet car, situated toward the rear of the train," and five minutes after we pulled out a boy came to sit beside me on my right: one of the sons of the town, eating from a cardboard box a grayish pad of meat which shined his fingers with fat.

WHEN I ARRIVED home, I threw my bag into a corner as if I hated it, and standing in the kitchen—last night's washing up not done, and two wineglasses, I noticed—I ate a single cheese cracker dry out of the tin. Back to work, I thought. Sit down and type. Or you might just die of a surfeit.

In the next few weeks, my biography took some unexpected turns. Aunt Virginie and the Mexican got into the text quite a lot. I began to make versions in which Aunt Virginie and the Mexican ran off together, and in which (therefore) my subject had never been born. I could see them speeding across Europe on an adulterous spree, accompanied by the sound of shattering glass: drinking spa towns dry of champagne and breaking the bank at Monte Carlo. I made up that the Mexican went home with the proceeds and led a successful revolution, with Aunt Virginie featuring in it as a sort of La Pasionaria figure: but with dancing, as if Isadora Duncan had got into it some-how. It was all very different from my previous work.

IN THE EARLY autumn of that year, three months after my trip east, I was at Waterloo Station, on my way to give a talk at a branch library in Hampshire. I had no opinion, now, of the catering anywhere in England. As I turned from the sandwich counter, balancing a baguette I meant to carry carefully to Alton, a tall young man bumped into me and knocked my purse flying from my hand.

It was a full purse, bulging with change, and the coins

went wheeling and flying among the feet of fellow travelers, spinning and scattering over the slippery floor. My luck was in, because the people streaming through from Eurostar began laughing and chasing my small fortune, making it a sport to chase every penny and trap it: perhaps they thought it was converse begging, or some sort of London custom, like Pearly Kings. The young man himself bobbed and weaved among the European feet, and eventually it was he who emptied a handful of change back into my purse, with a wide white smile, and, just for a second, pressed my hand to reassure me. Amazed, I gazed up into his face: he had large blue eyes, a shy yet confident set to him; he was six foot and lightly bronzed, strong but softly polite, his jacket of indigo linen artfully crumpled, his shirt a dazzling white; he was, in all, so clean, so sweet, so golden, that I backed off, afraid he must be American and about to convert me to some cult.

When I arrived at the library, an ambitious number of chairs—fifteen, at first count—were drawn up in a semicircle. Most were filled: a quiet triumph, no? I did my act on autopilot, except that when it came to my influences I went a bit wild and invented a Portuguese writer who I said knocked Pessoa into a cocked hat. The golden young man kept invading my mind, and I thought I'd quite like to go to bed with someone of that ilk, by way of a change. Wasn't everybody due a change? But he was a different order of being from me: a person on another plane. As the evening wore on, I began to feel chilly, and exposed, as if a wind were whistling through my bones.

I SAT UP for a while, in a good enough bed in a clean enough room, reading *The Right Side of Midnight*, making marginal annotations, and wondering why I'd ever thought the public might like it. My cheek burned on a lumpy pillow, and the usual images of failure invaded me; but then, about three o'clock I must have slept.

I woke refreshed, from no dreams: in a cider-apple dawn, a fizz and sharpness in the air. Out of bed, I rejoiced to see that someone had scrubbed the shower. I could bear to step into it, and did. Cold soft water ran over my scalp. My eyes stretched wide open. What was this? A turning point?

I was on the crowded train for eight, my fingers already twitching for my notebook. We had scarcely pulled out of the station when a grinning young steward bounced a laden trolley down the aisle. Seeing his Ginormous Harvest Cookies, his Golden Toastie Crunches in cellophane wrap, the men around me flapped their copies of the *Financial Times* at him, and began to jab their fingers, chattering excitedly. "Tea?" the steward exclaimed. "My pleasure, sir! Small or large?"

I noticed Large was just Small with more water, but I was swept away, infused by the general bonhomie. I took out my purse, and when I opened it I saw with surprise that the Queen's heads were tidily stacked, pointing upward. And was there one more head than I'd expected? I frowned. My fingers flicked the edges of the notes. I'd left home with eighty pounds. It seemed I was coming back with a round hundred. I was puzzled (as the steward handed me my Large Tea); but only for a moment. I remembered the young man with his broad white smile and his ashen hair streaked with gold; the basted perfection of his firm flesh, and the grace of his hand clasping mine. I slotted the notes back inside, slid my purse away, and wondered: which of my defects did he notice first?

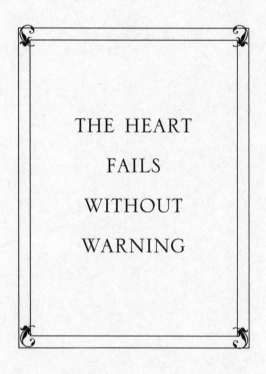

THE HEART

FAILS

WITHOUT

WARNING

September: When she began to lose weight at first, her sister had said, I don't mind; the less of her the better, she said. It was only when Morna grew hair—fine down on her face, in the hollow curve of her back—that Lola began to complain. I draw the line at hair, she said. This is a girls' bedroom, not a dog kennel.

Lola's grievance was this: Morna was born before she was, already she had used up three years' worth of air, and taken space in the world that Lola could have occupied. She believed she was birthed into her sister's squalling, her incessant *I-want I-want*, her *give-me give-me*.

Now Morna was shrinking, as if her sister had put a spell on her to vanish. She said, if Morna hadn't always been so greedy before, she wouldn't be like this now. She wanted everything.

Their mother said, "You don't know anything about it, Lola. Morna was not greedy. She was always picky about her food."

"Picky?" Lola made a face. If Morna didn't like something she would make her feelings known by vomiting it up in a weak acid dribble.

It's because of the school catchment area they have to live in a too-small house and share a bedroom. "It's bunk beds or GCSEs!" their mother said. She stopped, confused by herself. Often what she said meant something else entirely, but they were used to it; early menopause, Morna said. "You know what I mean," she urged them. "We live in this house for the sake of your futures. It's a sacrifice now for all of us, but it will pay off. There's no point in getting up every morning in a lovely room of your own and going to a sink school where girls get raped in the toilets."

"Does that happen?" Lola said. "I didn't know that happened."

"She exaggerates," their father said. He seldom said anything, so it made Lola jump, him speaking like that.

"But you know what I'm saying," her mother said. "I see them dragging home at two in the afternoon, they can't keep them in school. They've got piercings. There's drugs. There's internet bullying."

"We have that at our school," Lola said.

"It's everywhere," their father said. "Which is another reason to keep off the internet. Lola, are you listening to what I'm telling you?"

The sisters were no longer allowed a computer in their room because of the sites Morna liked to look at. They had pictures of girls with their arms stretched wide over their heads in a posture of crucifixion. Their ribs were spaced wide apart like the bars of oven shelves. These sites advised Morna how to be hungry, how not to be gross. Any food like bread, butter, an egg, is gross. A green apple or a green leaf, you may have one a day. The apple must be poison green. The leaf must be bitter.

"To me it is simple," their father said. "Calories in, calories out. All she has to do is open her mouth and put the food in, then swallow. Don't tell me she can't. It's a question of won't."

Lola picked up an eggy spoon from the draining board. She held it under her father's nose as if it were a microphone. "Yes, and have you anything you want to add to that?"

He said, "You'll never get a boyfriend if you look like a needle." When Morna said she didn't want a boyfriend, he shouted, "Tell me that again when you're seventeen."

. I never will be, Morna said. Seventeen.

SEPTEMBER: LOLA ASKED for the carpet to be replaced in their room. "Maybe we could have a wood floor? Easier to clean up after her?"

Their mother said, "Don't be silly. She's sick in the loo. Isn't she? Mostly? Though not," she said hurriedly, "like she used to be." It's what they had to believe: that Morna was getting better. In the night, you could hear them telling each other, droning on behind their closed bedroom door; Lola lay awake listening.

Lola said, "If I can't have a new carpet, if I can't have a wood floor, what can I have? Can I have a dog?"

"You are so selfish, Lola," their mother shouted. "How can we take on a pet at a time like this?"

Morna said, "If I die, I want a woodland burial. You can plant a tree and when it grows you can visit it."

"Yeah. Right. I'll bring my dog," Lola said.

SEPTEMBER: LOLA SAID, "The only thing is, now she's gone so small I can't steal her clothes. This was my main way of annoying her and now I have to find another."

All year round Morna wore wool to protect her shoulders, elbows, hips, from the blows of the furniture, and also to look respectably fat so that people didn't point her out on the street; also, because even in July she was cold. But the winter came early for her, and though the sun shone outside she was getting into her underlayers. When she stepped on the scale for scrutiny she appeared to be wearing normal clothes, but actually she had provided herself with extra weight. She would wear one pair of tights over another; every gram counts, she told Lola. She had to be weighed every day. Their mother did it. She would try surprising Morna with spot checks, but Morna would always know when she was getting into a weighing mood.

Lola watched as their mother pulled at her sister's cardigan, trying to get it off her before she stepped onto the scales. They tussled like two little kids in a playground; Lola screamed with laughter. Their mother hauled at the sleeve and Morna shouted, "Ow, ow!" as if it were her skin being stretched. Her skin was loose, Lola saw. Like last year's school uniform, it was too big for her. It didn't matter, because the school had made it clear they didn't want to see her this term. Not until she's turned the corner, they said, on her way back to a normal weight. Because the school has such a competitive ethos. And it could lead to mass fatalities if the girls decided to compete with Morna.

When the weighing was over, Morna would come

into their bedroom and start peeling off her layers, while Lola watched her, crouched on her bottom bunk. Morna would stand sideways to the mirror with her ribs arched. You can count them, she said. After the weighing she needed reassurance. Their mother bought them the long mirror because she thought Morna would be ashamed when she saw herself. The opposite was true.

OCTOBER: IN THE morning paper there was a picture of a skeleton. "Oh look," Lola said, "a relative of yours." She pushed it across the breakfast table to where Morna sat poking a Shredded Wheat with her spoon, urging it toward disintegration. "Look, Mum! They've dug up an original woman."

"Where?" Morna said. Lola read aloud, her mouth full. "Ardi stands four feet high. She's called Ardipithecus. Ardi for short. For short!" She spluttered at her own joke, and orange juice came down her nose. "They've newly discovered her. 'Her brain was the size of a chimpanzee's.' That's like you, Morna. 'Ardi weighed about fifty kilograms.' I expect that was when she was wearing all her animal skins, not when she was just in her bones."

"Shut it, Lola," their father said. But then he got up and walked out, breakfast abandoned, his mobile phone in his hand. His dirty knife, dropped askew on his plate, swung across the disk like the needle of a compass, and rattled to its rest. Always he was no more than a shadow in their lives. He worked all the hours, he said, to keep the small house going, worrying about the mortgage and the car while all *she* worried about was her bloody waistline.

Lola looked after him, then returned to the original woman. "Her teeth show her diet was figs. 'She also ate leaves and small mammals.' Yuck, can you believe that?"

"Lola, eat your toast," their mother said.

"They found her in bits and pieces. First just a tooth. 'Fossil hunters first glimpsed this species in 1992.' That's just before we first glimpsed Morna."

"Who found her?" Morna said.

"Lots of people. I told you, they found her in bits. 'Fifteen years' work involving forty-seven researchers.'"

Looking at Morna, their mother said, "You were fifteen years' work. Nearly. And there was only me to do it."

"'She was capable of walking upright,'" Lola read. "So are you, Morna. Till your bones crumble. You'll look like an old lady." She stuffed her toast into her mouth. "But not four million years old."

NOVEMBER: ONE MORNING their mother caught Morna knocking back a jug of water before the weigh-in. She shouted, "It can swell your brain! It can kill you!" She knocked the jug out of her daughter's hand and it shattered all over the bathroom floor.

She said, "Oh, seven years' bad luck. No, wait. That's mirrors."

Morna wiped the back of her hand across her mouth. You could see the bones in it. She was like a piece of science course work, Lola said thoughtfully. Soon she'd have no personhood left. She'd be reduced to biology.

The whole household, for months now, a year, had been enmeshed in mutual deception. Their mother would make Morna a scrambled egg and slide a spoonful of double cream into it. The unit where Morna was an inpatient used to make her eat white-bread sandwiches thickly buttered and layered with rubber wedges of yellow cheese. She used to sit before them, hour after hour, compressing the bread under her hand to try to squeeze out the oily fat onto the plate. They would say, try a little, Morna. She would say, I'd rather die.

If her weight fell by a certain percentage she would have to go back to the unit. At the unit they stood over her until she ate. Meals were timed and had to be completed by the clock or there were penalties. The staff would watch her to make sure she was not slipping any food into the layers of her clothes, and layers in fact were monitored. There was a camera in every bathroom, or so Morna said. They would see her if she made herself sick. Then they would put her to bed. She lay so many days in bed that when she came home her legs were wasted and white.

The founder of the unit, a Scottish doctor with a burning ideal, had given the girls garden plots and required them to grow their own vegetables. Once she had seen a starving girl eat some young peas, pod and all. The sight had moved her, the sight of the girl stretching her cracked lips and superimposing the green, tender smile: biting down. If they only saw, she said, the good food come out of God's good earth.

But sometimes the girls were too weak for weeding and pitched forward into their plots. And they were picked up, brushing crumbs of soil away; the rakes and hoes lay abandoned on the ground, like weapons left on a battlefield after the defeat of an army.

NOVEMBER: THEIR MOTHER was grumbling because the supermarket van had not come with the order. "They say delivery in a two-hour time slot to suit you." She pulled open the freezer and rummaged. "I need parsley and yellow haddock for the fish pie."

Lola said, "It will look as if Morna's sicked it already."

Their mother yelled, "You heartless little bitch." Iced vapor billowed around her. "It's you who brings the unhappiness into this house."

Lola said, "Oh, is it?"

Last night Lola had seen Morna slide down from her bunk, a wavering column in the cold; the central heating was in its off phase, since no warm-blooded human being should be walking about at such an hour. She pushed back her quilt, stood up and followed Morna onto the dark landing. They were both barefoot. Morna wore a ruffled nightshirt, like a wraith in a story by Edgar Allan Poe. Lola wore her old Mr. Men pajamas, ages 8–9, to which she was attached beyond the power of reason. Mr. Lazy, almost washed away, was a faded smudge on the shrunken top, which rose and gaped over her round little belly; the pajama legs came halfway down her calves, and the elastic had gone at the waist, so she had to hitch herself together every few steps. There was a half moon and on the landing she saw her sister's face, bleached out, shadowed like the moon, cratered like the moon, mysterious and far away. Morna was on her way downstairs to the computer to cancel the supermarket order.

In their father's office Morna had sat down on his desk chair. She scuffed her bare heels on the carpet to wheel it up to the desk. The computer was for their father's work use. They had been warned of this and told their mother got ten GCSEs without the need of anything but a pen and paper; that they may use the computer under strict supervision; that they may also go online at the public library.

Morna got up the food order onscreen. She mouthed at her sister, "Don't tell her."

She'd find out soon enough. The food would come anyway. It always did. Morna didn't seem able to learn that. She said to Lola, "How can you bear to be so fat? You're only eleven."

Lola watched her as she sat with her face intent, patiently fishing for the forbidden sites, swaying backward and forward, rocking on the wheeled chair. She turned to go back to bed, grabbing her waist to stop her pajama bottoms from falling down. She heard a sound from her sister, a sound of something, she didn't know what. She turned back. "Morna? What's that?"

For a minute they didn't know what it was they were seeing on the screen: human or animal? They saw that it was a human, female. She was on all fours. She was naked. Around her neck there was a metal collar. Attached to it was a chain.

Lola stood, her mouth ajar, holding up her pajamas with both hands. A man was standing out of sight holding the chain. His shadow was on the wall. The woman looked like a whippet. Her body was stark white. Her face was blurred and wore no readable human expression. You couldn't recognize her. She might be someone you knew.

"Play it," Lola said. "Go on."

Morna's finger hesitated. "Working! He's always in here, working." She glanced at her sister. "Stick with Mr. Lazy, you'll be safer with him."

"Go on," Lola said. "Let's see."

But Morna erased the image. The screen was momentarily dark. One hand rubbed itself across her ribs, where her heart was. The other hovered over the keyboard; she retrieved the food order. She ran her eyes over it and added own-brand dog food. "I'll get the blame," Lola said. "For my fantasy pet." Morna shrugged.

Later they lay on their backs and murmured into the

dark, the way they used to do when they were little. Morna said he would claim he found it by accident. That could be the truth, Lola said, but Morna was quiet. Lola wondered if their mother knew. She said, you can get the police coming round. What if they come and arrest him? If he has to go to prison we won't have any money.

Morna said, "It's not a crime. Dogs. Women undressed as dogs. Only if it's children, I think that's a crime."

Lola said, "Does she get money for doing it or do they make her?"

"Or she gets drugs. Silly bitch!" Morna was angry with the woman or girl who for money or out of fear crouched like an animal, waiting to have her body despoiled. "I'm cold," she said, and Lola could hear her teeth chattering. She was taken like this, seized by cold that swept right through her body to her organs inside; her heart knocked, a marble heart. She put her hand over it. She folded herself in the bed, knees to her chin.

"If they send him to prison," Lola said, "you can earn money for us. You can go in a freak show."

* * *

NOVEMBER: DR. BHATTACHARYA from the unit came to discuss the hairiness. It happens, she said. The name of the substance is lanugo. Oh, it happens, I am afraid to say. She sat on the sofa and said, "With your daughter I am at my wits' end."

Their father wanted Morna to go back to the unit. "I would go so far as to say," he said, "either she goes, or I go."

Dr. Bhattacharya blinked from behind her spectacles. "Our funding is in a parlous state. From now till next financial year we are rationed. The most urgent referrals only. Keep up the good work with the daily weight chart. As long as she is stable and not losing. In spring if progress is not good we will be able to take her in."

Morna sat on the sofa, her arms crossed over her belly, which was swollen. She looked vacantly about her. She would rather be anywhere than here. It contaminates everything, she had explained, that deceitful spoonful of cream. She could no longer trust her food to be what it said it was, nor do her calorie charts if her diet was tampered with. She had agreed to eat, but others had broken the agreement. In spirit, she said.

Their father told the doctor, "It's no use saying all the time," he mimicked her voice, "'Morna, what do you think, what do you want?' You don't give me all this shit about human rights. It doesn't matter what she thinks anymore. When she looks in a mirror God knows what she sees. You can't get hold of it, can you, what goes on in that head of hers? She imagines things that aren't there."

Lola jumped in. "But I saw it too."

Her parents rounded on her. "Lola, go upstairs."

She flounced up from the sofa and went out, dragging her feet. They didn't say, "See what, Lola? What did you see?"

They don't listen, she had told the doctor, to anything I say. To them I am just noise. "I asked for a pet, but no, no chance—other people can have a dog, but not Lola."

Expelled from the room, she stood outside the closed door, whimpering. Once she scratched with her paw. She snuffled. She pushed at the door with her shoulder, a dull bump, bump.

"Family therapy may be available," she heard Dr. Bhattacharya say. "Had you thought of that?"

* * *

DECEMBER: Merry Christmas.

JANUARY: "YOU'RE GOING to send me back to the unit," Morna said.

"No, no," her mother said. "Not at all."

"You were on the phone to Dr. Bhattacharya."

"I was on the phone to the dentist. Booking in."

Morna had lost some teeth lately, this was true. But she knew her mother was lying. "If you send me back I will drink bleach," she said.

Lola said, "You will be shining white."

FEBRUARY: THEY TALKED about sectioning her: that means, their mother said, compulsory detention in a hospital, that means you will not be able to walk out, Morna, like you did before.

"It's entirely your choice," their father said. "Start eating, Morna, and it won't come to that. You won't like it in the loony bin. They won't be coaxing you out on walks and baking you bloody fairy cakes. They'll have locks on the doors and they'll be sticking you full of drugs. It won't be like the unit, I'm telling you."

"More like a boarding kennel, I should think," Lola said. "They'll be kept on leads."

"Won't you save me?" Morna said.

"You have to save yourself," their father said. "Nobody can eat for you."

"If they could," said Lola, "maybe I'd do it. But I'd charge a fee."

Morna was undoing herself. She was reverting to unbeing. Lola was her interpreter, who spoke out from the top bunk in the clear voice of a prophetess. They had to come to her, parents and doctors, to know what Morna thought. Morna herself was largely mute.

She had made Morna change places and sleep on the bottom bunk since new year. She was afraid Morna would roll out and smash herself on the floor.

She heard her mother moaning behind the bedroom door: "She's going, she's going."

She didn't mean "going to the shops." In the end, Dr. Bhattacharya had said, the heart fails without warning.

FEBRUARY: AT THE last push, in the last ditch, she decided to save her sister. She made her little parcels wrapped in tinfoil—a single biscuit, a few pick'n'mix sweets—and left them on her bed. She found the biscuit, still in its foil, crushed to crumbs, and on the floor of their room shavings of fudge and the offcut limbs of pink jelly lobsters. She could not count the crumbs, so she hoped Morna was eating a little. One day she found Morna holding the foil, uncrumpled, looking for her reflection in the shiny side. Her sister had double vision now, and solid objects were ringed by light; they had a ghost-self, fuzzy, shifting.

Their mother said, "Don't you have any feelings, Lola? Have you no idea what we're going through, about your sister?"

"I had some feelings," Lola says. She held out her hands in a curve around herself, to show how emotion distends you. It makes you feel full up, a big weight in your chest, and then you don't want your dinner. So she had begun to leave it, or surreptitiously shuffle bits of food—pastry, an extra potato—into a piece of kitchen roll.

She remembered that night in November when they went barefoot down to the computer. Standing behind Morna's chair, she had touched her shoulder, and it was like grazing a knife. The blade of the bone seemed to sink deep into her hand, and she felt it for hours; she was surprised not to see the indent in her palm. When she had woken up next morning, the shape of it was still there in her mind.

MARCH: ALL TRACES of Morna have gone from the bedroom now, but Lola knows she is still about. These cold nights, her Mr. Men pajamas hitched up with one hand, she stands looking out over the garden of the small house. By the lights of hovering helicopters, by the flash of the security lights from neighboring gardens, by the backlit flicker of the streets, she sees the figure of her sister standing and looking up at the house, bathed in a nimbus of frost. The traffic flows long into the night, a hum without ceasing, but around Morna there is a bubble of quiet. Her tall straight body flickers inside her nightshirt, her face is blurred as if from tears or drizzle, and she wears no readable human expression. But at her feet a white dog lies, shining like a unicorn, a golden chain about its neck.

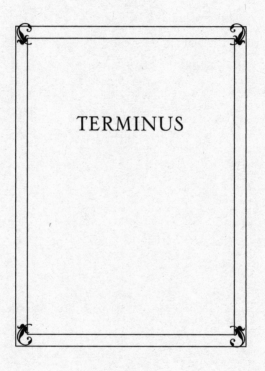

TERMINUS

On January 9th, shortly after eleven on a dark sleety morning, I saw my dead father on a train pulling out of Clapham Junction, bound for Waterloo.

I glanced away, not recognizing him at once. We were on parallel tracks. When I looked back, the train had picked up speed, and carried him away.

My mind at once moved ahead, to the concourse at Waterloo Station, and the meeting which I felt sure must occur. The train on which he was traveling was one of the old six-seater carriage-and-corridor type, its windows near-opaque with the winter's accumulation, and a decade of grime plastered to its metal. I wondered where he'd come from: Windsor? Ascot? You'll understand that I travel in the region a good deal, and one gets to know the rolling stock.

There were no lights in the carriage he had chosen. (The bulbs are often stolen or vandalized.) His face had an unpleasant tinge; his eyes were deeply shadowed, and his expression was thoughtful, almost morose.

At last released by the green signal, my own train began to draw forward. Its pace was stately and I thought that he must have a good seven minutes on me, certainly more than five.

As soon as I saw him, sitting sad but upright in that opposite carriage, my mind went back to the occasion when . . . to the occasion when . . . But no. It did not go back. I tried, but I could not find an occasion. Even when I scrubbed the recesses of my brain, I could not scour one out. I should like to be rich in anecdote. Fertile to invent. But there's no occasion, only the knowledge that a certain number of years have passed.

When we disembarked the platform was slick with

cold, sliding underfoot. The bomb warnings were pasted
up everywhere, also the beggar warnings, and posters saying take care not to slip or trip, which are insulting to the
public, as few people would do it if they could help it:
only some perhaps, a few attention seekers. An arbitrary
decision had placed a man to take tickets, so that was fum-
bling, and further delay. I was irritated by this; I wanted to
get on with the whole business, whatever the business was
going to be.

It came to me that he had looked younger, as though
death had moved him back a stage. There had been in his
expression, melancholy though it was, something purpo-
sive; and I was sure of this, that his journey was not random. And so it was this perception, rather than any past
experience—is experience always past?—that made me
think he might linger for a rendezvous, that moving
toward me and then away, on his Basingstoke train or perhaps from as far as Southampton, he might make time for
a meeting with me.

I tell you this: if you are minded to unite at Waterloo
Station, lay your plans well and in advance. Formalize in

writing, for extra caution. I stood still, a stone in the rude stream, as the travelers crashed and surged around me. Where might he go? What might he want? (I had not known, God help me, that the dead were loose.) A cup of coffee? A glance at the rack of best-selling paperbacks? An item from Boots the Chemist, a cold cure, a bottle of some aromatic oil?

Something small and hard, that was inside my chest, that was my heart, drew smaller then. I had no idea what he would want. The limitless possibilities that London affords . . . if he should bypass me and find his way into the city . . . but even then, among the limitless possibilities, I could not think of a single thing that he might want.

SO I HUNTED for him, peeping into W. H. Smith and the Costa Coffee boutique. My mind tried to provide occasions to which it could go back, but none occurred. I coveted something sweet, a glass of hot chocolate to warm my hands, an Italian wafer dusted with cocoa powder. But my mind was cold and my intention urgent.

It struck me that he might be leaving for the Continent. He could take the train from here to Europe, and how would I follow? I wondered what documents he would be likely to need, and whether he bore currency. Are dispensations different? As ghosts, can they pass the ports? I thought of a court of shadow ambassadors, with shadow portfolios tucked within their silks.

There is a rhythm—and you know this—to which people move in any great public space. There is a certain speed that is no one's decision, but is set going every day, soon after dawn. Break the rhythm and you'll rue it, for you'll be kicked and elbows will collide. Brutal British mutter of sorry, oh sorry—except often travelers are too angry I find for common politeness, hesitate too long or limp and you will be knocked out of the way. It occurred to me for the first time that this rhythm is a mystery indeed, controlled not by the railways or the citizens but by a higher power: that it is an aid to dissimulation, a guide to those who would otherwise not know how to act.

For how many of all these surging thousands are solid, and how many of these assumptions are tricks of the light?

How many, I ask you, are connected at all points, how many are utterly and convincingly in the state they purport to be: which is, alive? That lost, objectless, sallow man, a foreigner with his bag on his back; that woman whose starved face recalls a plague-pit victim? Those dwellers in the brown houses of Wandsworth, those denizens of balcony flats and walkways; those grumbling commuters gathered for Virginia Water, those whose homes perch on embankments, or whose roofs glossy with rain fly away from the traveler's window? How many?

For distinguish me, will you? Distinguish me "the distinguished thing." Render me the texture of flesh. Pick me what it is, in the timbre of the voice, that marks out the living from the dead. Show me a bone that you know to be a living bone. Flourish it, will you? Find one, and show me.

MOVING ON, I stared over the chill cabinet with its embalmed meals for travelers. I caught a glimpse of a sleeve, of an overcoat which I thought might be familiar, and my narrow heart skipped sideways. But then the man turned, and his face was sodden with stupidity, and he was someone else, and less than I required him to be.

Not many places were left. I looked at the pizza stand, but I did not think he would eat in a public place, and not anything foreign. (Again my mind darted forward to the Gare du Nord and the chances of catching up.) The *bureau de change* I'd already checked, and had scooped aside the curtain of the photograph booth, which seemed empty at the time but I had thought it might be a trick or a test.

So nowhere then. Dwelling again on his expression—and you will remember I saw it only for a moment, and in shadows—I discerned something that I did not see at first. It seemed, almost, that his look was turning inward. There was a remoteness, a wish for privacy: as if he were the warden of his own identity.

Suddenly—the thought born in a second—I understood: he is traveling incognito. Shame and rage then made me lean back against plate glass, against the front window of a bookshop; aware that my own image swims behind me, and that my ghost, in its winter cloak, is forced into the glass, forced there and fixed for any passer to stare at, living or dead, as long as I have not strength or power to move. My morning's experience, till then unprocessed and scantily observed, now arrived inside me. I had raised my eyes, I had lifted my gaze, I had with naked curiosity looked into the carriage on the parallel track, and by indecent coincidence I had happened to see a thing I should never have seen.

It seemed urgent now to go into the city and to my meeting. I gathered my cloak about me, my customary suit of solemn black. I looked in my bag to pat that all my papers were in order. I went to a stall and handed over a pound coin, for which I was given a pack of paper handkerchiefs in a plastic sheath as thin as skin, and using my nails I tore it till the membrane parted, and the paper itself was under my hand: it was a provision, in case of unseemly tears. Though paper reassures me, its touch. It's what you respect.

This is a bleak winter. Even old people admit it is more frigid than the usual, and it is known that as you stand in the taxi queue the four winds sting your eyes. I am on my way to a chilly room, where men who might have been my father but more fond will resolve some resolutions, transact some transactions, agree on the minutes: I notice how easily, in most cases, committees agree the minutes, but when we are singular and living our separate lives we dispute—don't we?—each second we believe we own. It's not generally agreed, it's not much appreciated, that people are divided by all sorts of things, and that, frankly, death is the least of them. When lights are blossoming out across the boulevards and parks, and the town assumes its Victorian *sagesse*, I shall be moving on again. I see that both the living and the dead commute, riding their familiar trains. I am not, as you will have gathered, a person who needs false excitement, or simulated innovation. I am willing, though, to tear up the timetable and take some new routes; and I know I shall find, at some unlikely terminus, a hand that is meant to rest in mine.

THE

ASSASSINATION

OF MARGARET

THATCHER:

AUGUST 6TH 1983

Aᴘʀɪʟ 25ᴛʜ 1982, ᴅᴏᴡɴɪɴɢ sᴛʀᴇᴇᴛ:
Announcement of the recapture of South Georgia, in the
Falkland Islands.

Mrs. Thatcher: Ladies and gentlemen, the Secretary of
State for Defense has just come over to give me some very
good news . . .

Secretary of State: The message we have got is that British
troops landed on South Georgia this afternoon, shortly
after 4 p.m. London time . . . The commander of the

operation has sent the following message: "Be pleased to inform Her Majesty that the White Ensign flies alongside the Union Jack in South Georgia. God save the Queen."

Mrs. Thatcher: Just rejoice at that news and congratulate our forces and the marines. Good night, gentlemen.

Mrs. Thatcher turns toward the door of No. 10 Downing Street.

Reporter: Are we going to declare war on Argentina, Mrs. Thatcher?

Mrs. Thatcher (pausing on her doorstep): Rejoice.

Picture first the street where she breathed her last. It is a quiet street, sedate, shaded by old trees: a street of tall houses, their façades smooth as white icing, their brick-work the color of honey. Some are Georgian, flat-fronted. Others are Victorian, with gleaming bays. They are too big for modern households, and most of them have been cut up into flats. But this does not destroy their elegance of proportion, nor detract from the deep luster of paneled front doors, brass-furnished and painted in navy or forest green. It is the neighborhood's only drawback, that there are more cars than spaces to put them. The residents park nose-to-tail, flaunting their permits. Those who have driveways are often blocked into them. But they are patient householders, proud of their handsome street and willing to suffer to live there. Glancing up, you notice a fragile Georgian fanlight, or a warm scoop of terra-cotta tiling, or a glint of colored glass. In spring, cherry trees toss extravagant flounces of blossom. When the wind strips the petals, they flurry in pink drifts and carpet the pavements, as if giants have held a wedding in the street. In summer, music floats from open windows: Vivaldi, Mozart, Bach.

The street itself describes a gentle curve, joining the main road as it flows out of town. The Holy Trinity Church, islanded, is hung with garrison flags. Looking from a high window over the town (as I did that day of the killing) you feel the close presence of fortress and castle. Glance to your left, and the Round Tower looms into view, pressing itself against the panes. But on days of drizzle and drifting cloud the keep diminishes, like an amateur drawing half erased. Its lines soften, its edges fade; it shrinks into the raw cold from the river, more like a shrouded mountain than a castle built for kings.

The houses on the right-hand side of Trinity Place—I mean, on the right-hand side as you face out of town—have large gardens, each now shared between three or four tenants. In the early 1980s, England had not succumbed to the smell of burning. The carbonized reek of the weekend barbecue was unknown, except in the riverside gin palaces of Maidenhead and Bray. Our gardens, though immaculately kept, saw little footfall; there were no children in the street, just young couples who had yet to breed and older couples who might, at most, open a door to let an evening party spill out onto a terrace. Through warm afternoons the lawns baked unattended, and cats curled snoozing in the crumbling topsoil of stone urns. In autumn, leaf-heaps composted themselves on sunken patios, and were shoveled up by irritated owners of basement flats. The winter rains soaked the shrubberies, with no one there to see.

But in the summer of 1983 this genteel corner, bypassed by shoppers and tourists, found itself a focus of national interest. Behind the gardens of No. 20 and No. 21 stood the grounds of a private hospital, a graceful pale building occupying a corner site. Three days before her assassination, the prime minister entered this hospital for minor eye surgery. Since then, the area had been dislocated. Strangers jostled residents. Newspapermen and TV crews blocked the street and parked without permission in driveways. You would see them trundle up and down Spinner's Walk trailing wires and lights, their gaze rolling toward the hospital gates on Clarence Road, their necks noosed by camera straps. Every few minutes they would coagulate in a mass of heaving combat jackets, as if to reassure each other that nothing was happening: but that it would happen, by and by. They waited, and while they waited they slurped orange juice from cartons and lager from cans; they ate, crumbs spilling down their fronts, soiled paper bags chucked into flowerbeds. The baker at the top of St. Leonard's Road ran out of cheese rolls by 10 a.m. and everything else by noon. Windsorians clustered on Trinity Place, shopping bags wedged onto low walls. We speculated on why we had this honor, and when she might go away.

Windsor's not what you think. It has an intelligentsia. Once you wind down from the castle to the bottom of Peascod Street, they are not all royalist lickspittles; and as you cross over the junction to St. Leonard's Road, you might sniff out closet republicans. Still, it was cold comfort at the polls for the local socialists, and people murmured that it was a vote wasted; they had to show the strength of their feelings by tactical voting, and their spirit by attending outré events at the arts center. Recently remodeled from the fire station, it was a place where self-published poets found a platform, and sour white wine was dispensed from boxes; on Saturday mornings there were classes in self-assertion, yoga and picture framing.

But when Mrs. Thatcher came to visit, the dissidents took to the streets. They gathered in knots, inspecting the press corps and turning their shoulders to the hospital gates, where a row of precious parking bays were marked out and designated DOCTORS ONLY.

A woman said, "I have a PhD, and I'm often tempted to park there." It was early, and her loaf was still warm from the baker; she snuggled it against her, like a pet. She said, "There are some strong opinions flying about."

"Mine is a dagger," I said, "and it's flying straight to her heart."

"Your sentiment," she said admiringly, "is the strongest I've heard."

"Well, I have to go in," I said. "I'm expecting Mr. Duggan to mend my boiler."

"On a Saturday? Duggan? You're highly honored. Better scoot. If you miss him he'll charge you. He's a shark, that man. But what can you do?" She fished for a pen in the bottom of her bag. "I'll give you my number." She wrote it on my bare arm, as neither of us had paper. "Give me a ring. Do you ever go to the arts center? We can get together over a glass of wine."

I WAS PUTTING my Perrier water in the fridge when the doorbell rang. I'd been thinking, we don't know it now, but we'll look back with fondness on the time Mrs. Thatcher was here: new friendships formed in the street, chitchat about plumbers whom we hold in common. On the entryphone there was the usual crackle, as if someone had set fire to the line. "Come up, Mr. Duggan," I said. It was as well to be respectful to him.

I lived on the third floor, the stairs were steep and Duggan was ponderous. So I was surprised at how soon I heard the tap at the door. "Hello," I said. "Did you manage to park your van?"

On the landing—or rather on the top step, as I was alone up there—stood a man in a cheap quilted jacket. My innocent thought was, here is Duggan's son. "Boiler?" I said.

"Right," he said.

He heaved himself in, with his boiler man's bag. We were nose to nose in the box-sized hall. His jacket, more than adequate to the English summer, took up the space between us. I edged backward. "What's up with it?" he said.

"It groans and bangs. I know it's August, but—"

"No, you're right, you're right, you can never trust the weather. Rads hot?"

"In patches."

"Air in your system," he said. "While I'm waiting I'll bleed it. Might as well. If you've got a key."

It was then that a suspicion struck me. Waiting, he said. Waiting for what? "Are you a photographer?"

He didn't answer. He was patting himself down, searching his pockets, frowning.

"I was expecting a plumber. You shouldn't just walk in."

"You opened the door."

"Not to you. Anyway, I don't know why you bothered. You can't see the front gates from this side. You need to go out of here," I said pointedly, "and turn left."

"They say she's coming out the back way. It's a great place to get a shot."

My bedroom had a perfect view of the hospital garden; anyone, by walking around the side of the house, could guess this.

"Who do you work for?" I said.

"You don't need to know."

"Perhaps not, but it would be polite to tell me."

As I backed into the kitchen, he followed. The room was full of sunlight, and now I saw him clearly: a stocky man, thirties, unkempt, with a round friendly face and

THE ASSASSINATION OF MARGARET THATCHER

unruly hair. He dumped his bag on the table, and pulled off his jacket. His size diminished by half. "Let's say I'm freelance."

"Even so," I said, "I should get a fee for the use of my premises. It's only fair."

"You couldn't put a price on this," he said.

By his accent, he was from Liverpool. Far from Duggan, or Duggan's son. But then he hadn't spoken till he was in at the front door, so how could I have known? He could have been a plumber, I said to myself. I hadn't been a total fool; for the moment, self-respect was all that concerned me. Ask for identification, people advise, before letting a stranger in. But imagine the ruckus that Duggan would have caused, if you'd held his boy up on the stairs, impeding him from getting to the next boiler on his list, and shortening his plunder opportunities.

The kitchen window looked down over Trinity Place, now seething with people. If I craned my neck I could see a new police presence to my left, trotting up from the private gardens of Clarence Crescent. "Have one of these?" The visitor had found his cigarettes.

"No. And I'd rather you didn't."

"Fair enough." He crushed the pack into his pocket, and pulled out a balled-up handkerchief. He stood back from the tall window, mopping his face; face and handkerchief were both crumpled and gray. Clearly it wasn't something he was used to, tricking himself into private houses. I was more annoyed with myself than with him. He had a living to make, and perhaps you couldn't blame him for pushing in, when some fool of a woman held the door open. I said, "How long do you propose to stay?"

"She's expected in an hour."

"Right." That accounted for it, the increased hum and buzz from the street. "How do you know?"

"We've a girl on the inside. A nurse."

I handed him two sheets of kitchen roll. "Ta." He blotted his forehead. "She's going to come out and the doctors and nurses are lining up, so she can appreciate them. She's going to walk along the line with her thank-you and bye-bye, then toddle round the side, duck into a limo and she's away. Well, that's the idea. I don't have an exact time. So I thought if I was here early I could set up, have a look at the angles."

"How much will you get for a good shot?"

"Life without parole," he said.

I laughed. "It's not a crime."

"That's my feeling."

"It's a fair distance," I said. "I mean, I know you have special lenses, and you're the only one up here, but don't you want a close-up?"

"Nah," he said. "As long as I get a clear view, the distance is a doddle."

He crumpled up the kitchen roll and looked around for the bin. I took the paper from him, he grunted, then applied himself to unstrapping his bag, a canvas holdall that I supposed would be as suitable for a photographer as for any tradesman. But one by one he took out metal parts which, even in my ignorance, I knew were not part of a photographer's kit. He began to assemble them; his fingertips were delicate. As he worked he sang, almost under his breath, a little song from the football terraces:

You are a scouser, a dirty scouser,
You're only happy on giro day.
Your dad's out stealing, your mam's drug-dealing,
Please don't take our hub-caps away.

"Three million unemployed," he said. "Most of them live round our way. It wouldn't be a problem here, would it?"

"Oh no. Plenty of gift shops to employ everybody. Have you been up to the High Street?"

I thought of the tourist scrums pushing each other off the pavements, jostling for souvenir humbugs and windup Beefeaters. It could have been another country. No voices carried from the street below. Our man was humming, absorbed. I wondered if his song had a second verse. As he lifted each component from his bag he wiped it with a cloth that was cleaner than his handkerchief, handling it with gentle reverence, like an altar boy polishing the vessels for mass.

When the mechanism was assembled he held it out for my inspection. "Folding stock," he said. "That's the beauty of her. Fits in a cornflakes packet. They call her the widowmaker. Though not in this case. Poor bloody Denis, eh? He'll have to boil his own eggs from now on."

IT FEELS, IN retrospect, as if hours stretched ahead, as we sat in the bedroom together, he on a folding chair near the sash window, his mug of tea cradled in his hands, the widowmaker at his feet; myself on the edge of the bed, over which I had hastily dragged the duvet to tidy it. He had brought his jacket from the kitchen; perhaps the pockets were crammed with assassin's requisites. When he flung it on the bed, it slid straight off again. I tried to grab it and my palm slid across the nylon; like a reptile, it seemed to have its own life. I flumped it on the bed beside me and took a grip on it by the collar. He looked on with mild approval.

He kept glancing at his watch, though he said he had no certain time. Once he rubbed its face with his palm, as if it might be fogged and concealing a different time underneath. He would check, from the corner of his eye, that I was still where I should be, my hands in view: as, he explained, he preferred them to be. Then he would fix his gaze on the lawns, the back fences. As if to be closer to his target, he rocked his chair forward on its front legs.

I said, "It's the fake femininity I can't stand, and the counterfeit voice. The way she boasts about her dad the grocer and what he taught her, but you know she would change it all if she could, and be born to rich people. It's the way she loves the rich, the way she worships them. It's her philistinism, her ignorance, and the way she revels in her ignorance. It's her lack of pity. Why does she need an eye operation? Is it because she can't cry?"

When the telephone rang, it made us both jump. I broke off what I was saying. "Answer that," he said. "It will be for me."

IT WAS HARD for me to imagine the busy network of activity that lay behind the day's plans. "Wait," I'd said to him, as I asked him, "Tea or coffee?" as I switched the kettle on. "You know I was expecting the boiler man? I'm sure he'll be here soon."

"Duggan?" he said. "Nah."

"You know Duggan?"

"I know he won't be here."

"What have you done to him?"

"Oh, for God's sake." He snorted. "Why would we do anything? No need. He got the nod. We have pals all over the place."

Pals. A pleasing word. Almost archaic. Dear God, I thought, Duggan an IRA man. Not that my visitor had named his affiliation, but I had spoken it loudly in my mind. The word, the initials, didn't cause me the shock or upset it would cause, perhaps, to you. I told him this, as I reached in the fridge for milk and waited for the kettle to boil: saying, I would deter you if I could, but it would only be out of fear for myself and what's going to happen to me after you've done it: which by the way is what? I am no friend of this woman, though I don't (I felt compelled to add) believe violence solves anything. But I would not betray you, because . . .

"Yeah," he said. "Everybody's got an Irish granny. It's no guarantee of anything at all. I'm here for your sightlines. I don't care about your affinities. Keep away from the front window and don't touch the phone, or I'll knock you dead. I don't care about the songs your bloody great-uncles used to sing on a Saturday night."

I nodded. It was only what I'd thought myself. It was sentiment and no substance.

> *The minstrel boy to the war is gone,*
> *In the ranks of death you'll find him.*
> *His father's sword he has girded on,*
> *And his wild harp slung behind him.*

My great-uncles (and he was right about them) wouldn't have known a wild harp if it had sprung up and bitten their bottoms. Patriotism was only an excuse to get what they called pie-eyed, while their wives had tea and ginger nuts then recited the rosary in the back kitchen. The whole thing was an excuse: why we are oppressed. Why we are sat here being oppressed, while people from other tribes are hauling themselves up by their own ungodly efforts and buying three-piece suites. While we are rooted here going la-la-la auld Ireland (because at this distance in time the words escape us) our neighbors are patching their quarrels, losing their origins and moving on, to modern, nonsectarian forms of stigma, expressed in modern songs: you are a scouser, a dirty scouser. I'm not, personally. But the north is all the same to southerners. And in Berkshire and the Home Counties, all causes are the same, all ideas for which a person might care to die: they are nuisances, a breach of the peace, and likely to hold up the traffic or delay the trains.

"You seem to know about me," I said. I sounded resentful.

"As much as anybody would need to know. That's to say, not that you're anything special. You can be a help if you want, and if you don't want, we can do accordingly."

He spoke as if he had companions. He was only one man. But a bulky one, even without the jacket. Suppose I had been a true-blue Tory, or one of those devout souls who won't so much as crush an insect: I still wouldn't have tried anything tricky. As it was, he counted on me to be docile, or perhaps, despite his sneering, he trusted me to some small extent. Anyway, he let me follow him into the bedroom with my mug of tea. He carried his own tea in his left hand and his gun in his right. He left the roll of sticky tape and the handcuffs on the kitchen table, where he'd put them when they came out of his bag.

And now he let me pick up the phone extension from the bedside table, and hand it to him. I heard a woman's voice, young, timid and far away. You would not have thought she was in the hospital round the corner. "Brendan?" she said. I did not imagine that was his real name.

HE PUT DOWN the receiver so hard it clattered. "There's some friggin' hold-up. It'll be twenty minutes, she reckons. Or thirty, it could even be thirty." He let his breath out, as if he'd been holding it since he stomped upstairs. "Bugger this. Where's the lav?"

You can surprise a person with *affinity*, I thought, and then say, "Where's the lav?" Not a Windsor expression. It wasn't really a question, either. The flat was so small that its layout was obvious. He took his weapon with him. I listened to him urinate. Run a tap. I heard splashing. I heard him come out, zipping his trousers. His face was red where he'd been toweling it. He sat down hard on the folding chair. There was a bleat from the fragile canework. He said, "You've got a number written on your arm."

"Yes."

"What's it a number of?"

"A woman." I dabbed my forefinger with my tongue and slicked it across the ink.

"You won't get it off that way. You need to get some soap and give it a good scrub."

"How kind of you to take an interest."

"Have you wrote it down? Her number?"

"No."

"Don't you want it?"

Only if I have a future, I thought. I wondered when it would be appropriate to ask.

"Make us another brew. And put sugar in it this time."

"Oh," I said. I was flustered by a failing in hospitality. "I didn't know you took sugar. I might not have white."

"The bourgeoisie, eh?"

I was angry. "You're not too proud to shoot out of my bourgeois sash window, are you?"

He lurched forward, hand groping for the gun. It wasn't to shoot me, though my heart leapt. He glared down into the gardens, tensing as if he were going to butt his head through the glass. He made a small, dissatisfied grunt, and sat down again. "A bloody cat on the fence."

"I have demerara," I said. "I expect it tastes the same, when it's stirred in."

"You wouldn't think of shouting out of the kitchen window, would you?" he said. "Or trying to bolt down the stairs?"

"What, after all I've said?"

"You think you're on my side?" He was sweating again. "You don't know my side. Believe me, you have no idea."

It crossed my mind then he might not be a Provisional, but from one of the mad splinter groups you heard of. I was hardly in a position to quibble; the end result would be the same. But I said, "Bourgeoisie, what sort of polytechnic expression is that?"

I was insulting him, and I meant to. For those of tender years, I should explain that polytechnics were institutes of higher education, for the young who missed university entrance: for those who were bright enough to say *affinity*, but still wore cheap nylon coats.

He frowned. "Brew the tea."

"I don't think you should sneer at my great-uncles for being cod-Irish, if you talk in slogans you found in skips."

"It was a sort of a joke," he said.

"Oh. Well. Was it?" I was taken aback. "It looks as if I've no more sense of humor than she has."

I indicated, with my head, the lawns outside the window, where the prime minister was shortly to die.

"I don't fault her for not laughing," he said. "I won't fault her for that."

"You should. It's why she can't see how ridiculous she is."

"I wouldn't call her ridiculous," he said, mulish. "Cruel, wicked, but not ridiculous. What's there to laugh at?"

"All things human laugh," I said.

After some thought, he replied, "Jesus wept."

He smirked. I saw he had relaxed, knowing that because of the friggin' delay he wouldn't have to murder yet. "Mind you," I said, "she'd probably laugh if she were here. She'd laugh because she despises us. Look at your anorak. She despises your anorak. Look at my hair. She despises my hair."

He glanced up. He'd not looked at me before, not to see me; I was just the tea maker. "The way it just hangs there," I explained. "Instead of being in corrugations. I ought to have it washed and set. It ought to go in graduated rollers, she knows where she is with that sort of hair. And I don't like the way she walks. 'Toddles,' you said. 'She'll toddle round.' You had it right, there."

"What do you think this is about?" he said.

"Ireland."

He nodded. "And I want you to understand that. I'm not shooting her because she doesn't like the opera. Or because you don't care for—what in sod's name do you call it?—her accessories. It's not about her handbag. It's not about her hairdo. It's about Ireland. Only Ireland, right?"

"Oh, I don't know," I said. "You're a bit of a fake yourself, I think. You're no nearer the old country than I am. Your great-uncles didn't know the words either. So you might want supporting reasons. Adjuncts."

"I was brought up in a tradition," he said. "And look, it brings us here." He looked around, as if he didn't believe it: the crucial act of a dedicated life, ten minutes from now, with your back to a chipboard wardrobe glossed with white veneer; a pleated paper blind, an unmade bed, a strange woman, and your last tea with no sugar in it. "I think of those boys on hunger strike," he said, "the first of them dead almost two years to the day that she was first elected: did you know that? It took sixty-six days for Bobby to die. And nine other boys not far behind him. After you've starved yourself for about forty-five days they say it gets better. You stop dry-heaving and you can take water again. But that's your last chance, because after fifty days you can hardly see or hear. Your body digests itself. It eats itself in despair. You wonder she can't laugh? I see nothing to laugh at."

"What can I say?" I asked him. "I agree with everything you've said. You go and make the tea and I'll sit here and mind the gun."

For a moment, he seemed to consider it.

"You'd miss. You're not trained at all."

"How are you trained?"

"Targets."

"It's not like a live person. You might shoot the nurses. The doctors."

"I might, at that."

I heard his long, smoker's cough. "Oh, right, the tea," I said. "But you know another thing? They may have been blind at the end, but their eyes were open when they went into it. You can't force pity from a government like hers. Why would she negotiate? Why would you expect it? What's a dozen Irishmen to them? What's a hundred? All those people, they're capital punishers. They pretend to be modern, but leave them to themselves and they'd gouge eyes out in the public squares."

"It might not be a bad thing," he said. "Hanging. In some circumstances."

I stared at him. "For an Irish martyr? Okay. Quicker than starving yourself."

"It is that. I can't fault you there."

"You know what men say, in the pub? They say, name an Irish martyr. They say, go on, go on, you can't, can you?"

"I could give you a string of names," he said. "They were in the paper. Two years, is that too long to remember?"

"No. But keep up, will you? The people who say this, they're Englishmen."

"You're right. They're Englishmen," he said sadly. "They can't remember bugger all."

TEN MINUTES, I thought. Ten minutes give or take. In defiance of him, I sidled up to the kitchen window. The street had fallen into its weekend torpor; the crowds were around the corner. They must be expecting her soon. There was a telephone on the kitchen worktop, right by my hand, but if I picked it up he would hear the bedroom extension give its little yip, and he would come out and kill me, not with a bullet but in some less obtrusive way that would not alert the neighbors and spoil his day.

I stood by the kettle while it boiled. I wondered: Has the eye surgery been a success? When she comes out, will she be able to see as normal? Will they have to lead her? Will her eyes be bandaged?

I did not like the picture in my mind. I called out to him, to know the answer. No, he shouted back, the old eyes will be sharp as a tack.

I thought, there's not a tear in her. Not for the mother in the rain at the bus stop, or the sailor burning in the sea. She sleeps four hours a night. She lives on the fumes of whiskey and the iron in the blood of her prey.

WHEN I TOOK back the second mug of tea, with the demerara stirred in, he had taken off his baggy sweater, which was unraveling at the cuffs; he dresses for the tomb, I thought, layer on layer but it won't keep out the cold. Under the wool he wore a faded flannel shirt. Its twisted collar curled up; I thought, he looks like a man who does his own laundry. "Hostages to fortune?" I said.

"No," he said, "I don't get very far with the lasses." He passed a hand over his hair to flatten it, as if the adjustment might change his fortunes. "No kids, well, none I know of."

I gave him his tea. He took a gulp and winced. "After . . ." he said.

"Yes?"

"Right after, they'll know where the shot's come from, it won't take any time for them to work that out. Once I get down the stairs and out the front door, they'll have me right there in the street. I'm going to take the gun, so as soon as they sight me they'll shoot me dead." He paused and then said, as if I had demurred, "It's the best way."

"Ah," I said. "I thought you had a plan. I mean, other than getting killed."

"What better plan could I have?" There was only a touch of sarcasm. "It's a godsend, this. The hospital. Your attic. Your window. You. It's cheap. It's clean. It gets the job done, and it costs one man."

I had said to him earlier, violence solves nothing. But it was only a piety, like a grace before meat. I wasn't attending to its meaning as I said it, and if I thought about it, I felt a hypocrite. It's only what the strong preach to the weak; you never hear it the other way round; the strong don't lay down their arms. "What if I could buy you a moment?" I said. "If you were to wear your jacket to the killing, and be ready to go: to leave the widowmaker here, and pick up your empty bag, and walk out like a boiler man, the way you came in?"

"As soon as I walk out of this house I'm done."

"But if you were to walk out of the house next door?"

"And how would that be managed?" he said.

I said, "Come with me."

HE WAS NERVOUS to leave it, his sentry post, but on this promise he must. We still have five minutes, I said, and you know it, so come, leave your gun tidily under your chair. He crowded up behind me in the hall, and I had to tell him to step back so I could open the door. "Put it on the latch," he advised. "It would be a farce if we were shut out on the stairs."

The staircases of these houses have no daylight. You can push a time switch on the wall and flood the landings with a yellow glare. After the allotted two minutes you will be back in the dark. But the darkness is not so deep as you first think.

You stand, breathing gently, evenly, eyes adapting. Feet noiseless on the thick carpets, descend just one half-flight. Listen: the house is silent. The tenants who share this staircase are gone all day. Closed doors annul and muffle the world outside, the cackle of news bulletins from radios, the buzz of the trippers from the top of the town, even the apocalyptic roar of the airplanes as they dip toward Heathrow. The air, uncirculated, has a camphor smell, as if the people who first lived here were creaking open wardrobes, lifting out their mourning clothes. Neither in nor out of the house, visible but not seen, you could lurk here for an hour undisturbed, you could loiter for a day. You could sleep here; you could dream. Neither innocent nor guilty, you could skulk here for decades, while the alderman's daughter grows old: between step and step, grow old yourself, slip the noose of your name. One day Trinity Place will fall down, in a puff of plaster and powdered bone. Time will draw to a zero point, a dot: angels will pick through the ruins, kicking up the petals from the gutters, arms wrapped in tattered flags.

On the stairs, a whispered word: "And will you kill me?" It is a question you can only ask in the dark.

"I'll leave you gagged and taped," he says. "In the kitchen. You can tell them I did it the minute I burst in."

"But when will you really do it?" Voice a murmur.

"Just before. No time after."

"You will not. I want to see. I'm not missing this."

"Then I'll tie you up in the bedroom, okay? I'll tie you up with a view."

"You could let me slip downstairs just before. I'll take a shopping bag. If nobody sees me go, I'll say I was out the whole time. But make sure to force my door, won't you? Like a break-in?"

"I see you know my job."

"I'm learning."

"I thought you wanted to see it happen."

"I'd be able to hear it. It'll be like the roar from the Roman circus."

"No. We'll not do that." A touch: hand brushing arm. "Show me this thing. Whatever it is I'm here for, wasting time."

On the half-landing there is a door. It looks like the door to a broom cupboard. But it is heavy. Heavy to pull, hand slipping on the brass knob.

"Fire door."

He leans past and yanks it open.

Behind it, two inches away, another door.

"Push."

He pushes. Slow glide, dark into matching dark. The same faint, trapped, accumulating scent, the scent of the margin where the private and public worlds meet: raindrops on contract carpet, wet umbrella, damp shoe-leather, metal tang of keys, the salt of metal in palm. But this is the house next door. Look down into the dim well. It is the same, but not. You can step out of that frame and into this. A killer, you enter No. 21. A plumber, you exit No. 20. Beyond the fire door there are other households with other lives. Different histories lie close; they are curled like winter animals, breathing shallow, pulse undetected.

What we need, it is clear, is to buy time. A few moments' grace to deliver us from a situation that seems unnegotiable. There is a quirk in the building's structure. It is a slender chance but the only one. From the house next door he will emerge a few yards nearer the end of the street: nearer the right end, away from town and castle, away from the crime. We must assume that despite his bravado he does not intend to die if he can help it: that somewhere in the surrounding streets, illegally parked in a resident's bay or blocking a resident's drive, there is a vehicle waiting for him, to convey him beyond reach, and dissolve him as if he had never been.

He hesitates, looking into the dark.

"Try it. Do not put on the light. Do not speak. Step through."

* * *

WHO HAS NOT seen the door in the wall? It is the invalid child's consolation, the prisoner's last hope. It is the easy exit for the dying man, who perishes not in the death grip of a rattling gasp but passes on a sigh, like a falling feather. It is a special door and obeys no laws that govern wood or iron. No locksmith can defeat it, no bailiff kick it in; patroling policemen pass it, because it is visible only to the eye of faith. Once through it, you return as angles and air, as sparks and flame. That the assassin was a flicker in its frame, you know. Beyond the fire door he melts, and this is how you've never seen him on the news. This is how you don't know his name, his face. This is how, to your certain knowledge, Mrs. Thatcher went on living till she died. But note the door: note the wall: note the power of the door in the wall that you never saw was there. And note the cold wind that blows through it, when you open it a crack. History could always have been otherwise. For there is the time, the place, the black opportunity: the day, the hour, the slant of the light, the ice-cream van chiming from a distant road near the bypass.

* * *

AND STEPPING BACK, into No. 21, the assassin grunts with laughter.

"Shh!" I say.

"Is that your great suggestion? They shoot me a bit further along the street? Okay, we'll give it a go. Exit along another line. A little surprise."

Time is short now. We return to the bedroom. He has not said if I shall live or should make other plans. He motions me to the window. "Open it now. Then get back."

He is afraid of a sudden noise that might startle someone below. But though the window is heavy, and sometimes shudders in its frame, the sash slides smoothly upward. He need not fret. The gardens are empty. But over in the hospital, beyond the fences and shrubs, there is movement. They are beginning to come out: not the official party, but a gaggle of nurses in their aprons and caps.

He takes up the widowmaker, lays her tenderly across his knees. He tips his chair forward, and because I see his hands are once more slippery with sweat I bring him a towel and he takes it without speaking, and wipes his palms. Once more I am reminded of something priestly: a sacrifice. A wasp dawdles over the sill. The scent of the gardens is watery, green. The tepid sunshine wobbles in, polishes his shabby brogues, moves shyly across the surface of the dressing table. I want to ask: When what is to happen, happens, will it be noisy? From where I sit? If I sit? Or stand? Stand where? At his shoulder? Perhaps I should kneel and pray.

And now we are seconds from the target. The terrace, the lawns, are twittering with hospital personnel. A receiving line has formed. Doctors, nurses, clerks. The chef joins it, in his whites and a toque. It is a kind of hat I have only seen in children's picture books. Despite myself, I giggle. I am conscious of every rise and fall of the assassin's breath. A hush falls: on the gardens, and on us.

High heels on the mossy path. Tippy-tap. Toddle on. She's making efforts, but getting nowhere very fast. The bag on the arm, slung like a shield. The tailored suit just as I have foreseen, the pussy-cat bow, a long loop of pearls, and—a new touch—big goggle glasses. Shading her, no doubt, from the trials of the afternoon. Hand extended, she is moving along the line. Now that we are here at last, there is all the time in the world. The gunman kneels, easing into position. He sees what I see, the glittering helmet of hair. He sees it shine like a gold coin in a gutter, he sees it big as the full moon. On the sill the wasp hovers, suspends itself in still air. One easy wink of the world's blind eye: "Rejoice," he says. "Fucking rejoice."

CREDITS

"The School of English" was first published in the *London Review of Books*, 2015.

"Sorry to Disturb" was first published (as "Sorry to Disturb: A Memoir") in the *London Review of Books*, 2009.

"Comma" was first published in the *Guardian*, 2010, and appeared in *The Best British Stories 2011* (Salt Publishing).

"The Long QT" was first published in the *Guardian*, 2012.

"Winter Break" was first published in *The Best British Stories 2011* (Salt Publishing) and appeared in the *Guardian*, 2012.

"Harley Street" was first published in *The Time Out Book of London Short Stories* (Penguin), 1993.

"Offences Against the Person" was first published in the *London Review of Books*, 2008.

"How Shall I Know You?" was first published in the *London Review of Books*, 2000.

"The Heart Fails Without Warning" was first published in the *Guardian*, 2009, and appeared in *Best European Fiction 2011* (Dalkey Archive Press).

"Terminus" was first published in the *London Review of Books*, 2004.